BARBARIAN'S
CHOICE

BARBARIAN'S CHOICE

This book is a work of fiction. I know, I know. Imagine that a book about big blue aliens is fiction, but it is. The names, characters, places, and incidents are products of the writer's imagination or have been used fictitiously and are not to be construed as real. Any resemblance to persons, living or dead, actual events, locales or organizations is entirely coincidental and would be pretty darn nifty.

www.RubyDixon.com

BARBARIAN'S CHOICE

ICE PLANET BARBARIANS

RUBY DIXON

CHAPTER 1

FARLI

"Come on, lazy one!" I say as I put my hands on my hips. "It is time to go out!" I tap my foot impatiently, though I am smiling. "If we linger here all morning all the good tree bark will be eaten, and then where will you be?"

Chahm-pee bleats at me, his expression stubborn as he puts his head in his favorite basket and continues eating his morning meal.

I groan and move forward, grabbing him by the harness Tee-fah-ni made for him. "Will it be like this today, then? Are we going to fight?"

He ignores me, head down as he chews. Some days Chahm-pee is eager to get out, but today he wishes to stay and eat and wallow in his laziness. I will not let him, though. He gets too fat in the brutal season, so during the bitter season, I make sure he hunts with me. "Move," I tell him, tugging on his harness and then giving his flank a slap.

Chahm-pee lifts his head and bares his yellow teeth at me,

showing he is displeased. I snort at this, because Chahm-pee is all show. He will bleat and drag his feet and then the moment we are in the sunlight, he is prancing and acting like a kit despite his age. At two hands of age—eight, by human count—Chahm-pee is full-grown and bigger than most dvisti. I think it is because I make sure he is well-fed. Probably too well-fed, if I go by my mother's advice. Kemli thinks I spend too much time focused on my pet and not enough on providing for the tribe. Perhaps she is right, but food has been plentiful ever since we came to Croatoan village, and Chahm-pee does not eat the same things we do.

I give another tug on his harness, but Chahm-pee weighs double what I do, and there is no budging him. He belches and puts his head back in his food basket.

I know what to get him to move, though. I sling my hunting pack over my shoulder and head toward the entrance to my hut, pretending like I am going to leave. "Mmmm," I say exaggeratedly, digging into my pocket. I carry a pouch of rakrak seeds—Chahm-pee's favorite—for such an occasion. I shake the bag and then pull it out.

His head immediately lifts, ears pricking. His little tail swishes back and forth. I have his attention now.

"So tasty," I coo, and head out of the hut a few steps, then wait.

The dvisti trots out behind me and noses my pocket. He knows what I have. Amused, I pull a few seeds out and let him eat them from my hand, and then continue to head out into the village. He follows behind me, like the well-trained animal I know he is not.

"Very good, my Chahm-pee," I tell him, pulling a few more seeds out of my pocket because I have a soft heart. "We shall go and get our hunting in for the day. That will be nice, will it not? We can enjoy the sunshine and the fresh air, and some fresh food to eat. We like fresh food, do we not?"

"Are you talking to Chompy again?" a woman calls out, laughter in her voice. "You know he still can't answer?"

I grin, ignoring Jo-see's teasing. Even though it is early, the village is bustling with tribesmates. Jo-see is herding her little family toward the longhouse, where Air-ee-aw-nuh will be teaching classes to the kits, like she does every day the hunters go out. When the weather is bad, that is family time. But when the day is crisp and sunny like today? The hunters head out into the wild and the kits head to class. Warrek teaches them hunting when they are older, but when they are little—and there are so, so many little ones in our tribe—Air-ee-aw-nuh teaches them to count and how to spell in the human language. She has offered to teach me, but I have too much to do. "Hello, Jo-see," I call out, smiling to the little mother. I wink at her small son, who is doing his best to squirm away from his mother's grip. "Hello, Joden."

"Farli, can I come with you?" Joden asks in his sweet little voice. "I want to play wif Chahm-pee."

"No, baby, you get to hang with Mommy and sissy today," Jo-see says in a calm voice, even as she adjusts the kit on her hip. Joha is only a season or so old, and sucks her thumb as she looks at me with big eyes. She is quiet and gentle, unlike her squirmy little brother. I wonder what their next kit will be like. Even now, Jo-see's belly is heavily rounded with yet another kit. The tribe loves to tease Haeden and his mate about their frequent resonances, but Haeden just takes it all in stride. I think he secretly loves the fact that he and his mate have resonated three times so quickly, but Jo-see loves being a mother and Haeden is a good father. They are happy.

And I sigh wistfully because I am envious of their happiness. "Where is your mate today?"

"Off spear-fishing with Hassen," Jo-see says, smiling. "It's a nice day and they said that means that the kas-fish will be emerging from the mud to warm themselves." Joden bends over and picks up a stick, his little tail swishing, and then offers it to his mother. She takes it without a glance, and her son scampers off to collect more things while his mother talks. Jo-see nods at me. "Going hunting yourself?"

I nod cheerily, watching Joden as he races over to Chahm-pee's side to pet him. The dvisti is huge full-grown, and while Joden is not afraid, he is still small in comparison and Chahm-pee has big feet. "This fat one needs to be fed, and I am filling that cache we emptied over the brutal season."

"Mm, well, be careful," Jo-see says as she shifts Joha in her arms. "Haeden said he saw tracks and to look out for metlaks. You know how dangerous they are."

I resist the urge to roll my eyes. Jo-see means well, but ever since Joden was born, she has tried to mother me—and everyone else in the tribe. No one has seen metlaks in this area for seasons, and I am as good a hunter as any. "I will."

"You taking Taushen with you? Or Sessah?"

I shake my head, trying to slide away from the conversation without being obvious. Jo-see loves to talk, and if given the chance, she will hold me here all morning without realizing it. "I did not ask them."

"Oh, you should," Stay-see says as she approaches. She holds Pacy's hand in hers and her second little son, Tash, is strapped in his carrier on her back. Pacy watches me with a curious look on his face. He is unlike Joden in that he is a quiet, thoughtful boy, whereas Joden is currently trying to pull Chahm-pee's tail.

I pry the little hands away from my pet and shake my head at Stay-see. "I have not seen them and do not want to wait around—"

"Sessah will be sad to miss you," Stay-see says in a sing-song voice, and Jo-see giggles.

I snort. Time to go, before they start matchmaking. "We must be going," I say firmly. "And these little hunters must be off to do their learning." I give Joden a conspiratorial wink and a pat, directing him back toward his waiting mother.

"Yeah, we're going to be late," Jo-see says, glancing over at Stay-see. "You feel like making breakfast this morning?"

"Don't I always?" Stay-see grins. "Harlow wanted us to stop by and get Rukhar along to class, too. You know he's a handful in the mornings."

Jo-see's flexible human brow creases. "She's still not feeling well?" When Stay-see shakes her head, I feel a bit of worry tug at me. All of the humans do well here despite the cold, except Har-loh. She has always been a bit fragile, but ever since resonating a second time to her mate, her pregnancy seems to be sucking the strength out of her. Every day she looks a little thinner, a little more faded as her belly grows. I know her mate is worried. I worry, too.

When I return, I will bring something special for Har-loh to make her smile, then. Maybe snowcat or the hraku roots the humans love so much. Perhaps that will help her spirits.

"I must be going," I tell them, but the two humans are barely paying attention, their minds focused on Har-loh or kits…or finding Sessah and foisting him off on me. I wave goodbye to the group and then grab Chahm-pee's harness and hurry him along before someone else can stop and talk to me. I like chatting with the human females, but I am more worried that Sessah is going to show up and ask to join me. We hurry along, and I am relieved that my dvisti is no longer dragging his hooves and trots after me eagerly. We make it out of the village and into the gorge alone, and once there, I can breathe a sigh of relief.

Sessah is…a problem, and one I do not know how to

handle. He is just coming into his adulthood and has decided that since we are closest in age, we should be pleasure-mates. I…do not share this sentiment. Sessah is nice, but he is also still gangly and young, and his adoring attentions make me uncomfortable. The tribe finds his devotion amusing, but I do not. I have taken no pleasure-mate since coming into my adulthood, and do not plan on it.

I am waiting for resonance.

Perhaps I am a dreamer, but I am waiting for a hunter that looks at me with fire in his belly and stars in his eyes. I want him to gaze at me the way Haeden gazes at Jo-see, or Pashov devours his Stay-see with his eyes. I want him to have that same intense look on his face like Hassen does when he watches Mah-dee, or Rukh when he cares for Har-loh. I want what Vektal and Shorshie have—to be his partner and equal in all ways, and to finish his thoughts for him, and to occasionally sneak away to do the mouth-matings when we think no one is looking.

I need a mate that will make my heart stir and my khui sing. And I know it is not Sessah. Nor is it Taushen, who has courted me in his own quiet way. I do not know who it will be yet, or if my mate is not yet born and I must wait endless hands of turns for him to grow into adulthood. Whatever it is, I am content to wait. My own mother is twenty-seven turns older than my father. It can happen, as long as I am patient.

I want everything to be perfect, and it will be.

"Farli," a voice calls out as I head toward the end of the canyon.

I turn, and it is my father, waving a leather-wrapped bundle in the air as he jogs after me. "Wait!"

"Father? You are not out hunting?" I greet him with a gentle clasp on the arm and press my cheek to his. "Is everything all right?"

"Everything is fine, Little Sunshine," my father says with a grin. He places the packet in my hand. "I am making sah-sah today and will go hunting later. As for this." He taps a finger on the packet. "Your mother did not want you to go out hunting without something to eat."

I roll my eyes and cannot resist a small giggle. I am my mother's youngest and she spoils me as if I am still a kit clinging to her skirts. "Tell her she has my thanks."

"Will you be out overnight? Rokan said the weather would be fair."

I shrug. "Possibly." It depends on how badly I need my space. I love to wander. Lately I have enjoyed going to the sand-covered beaches near the great salt lake, hoping to catch a glimpse of the green island that Jo-see swears was there so long ago. I have never seen it, and I think the earth-shake must have swallowed it. But I still like to look.

"Sessah was hunting for you this morning."

I grimace. "I might be gone a few days, actually."

He seems to understand, a slow smile spreading across his face. "Then be safe, and look out for metlaks."

"Always, Father." I hug him again and then wave goodbye as he heads back to the village and toward his waiting sah-sah pots. If Sessah is looking for me, then I will most certainly spend a bit longer out in the wild.

Chahm-pee bleats at me, as if agreeing…or just mad that I have not given him more seeds. I tuck the packet of food under my arm and offer my pet a few more treats. "Come, fat one. Let us get you on the pulley before Sessah comes this way."

Because we now live in a gorge instead of in a cave, there was no easy way for Chahm-pee to get in and out, nor the humans, who are not as good at climbing sheer surfaces as we sa-khui. Har-loh saved the day with one of her creations. She created a pulley that balances with some heavy weights on the other side. I do not know how it works, only that I harness Chahm-pee in on his rope-covered raft and get in beside him, and then I pull on the rope, hauling us both into the air without straining my arms. Once we get to the top, Chahm-pee waits until I unfasten him and then trots off onto the ledge. I jump off as well and then send the pulley back down again for the next person.

Now that we are back 'up,' the wind blasts into my face, ruffling my hair. I miss the wind and the sunlight down in the gorge. It is safe there, but it feels a bit like living in a hole on cloudy days. Today the suns are shining brightly, peeking out from behind the clouds, and the snow glistens blindingly bright. I give a happy sigh and close my eyes, drinking in the feeling. *I could live up here all the time,* I think. Just lie down in the snow and let the sunlight bake my bones.

I do not, of course. The day is wasting and already the suns are high in the sky. I do, however, strip off my tunic and my leathers until I am down to nothing but my loincloth and my boots. I stuff them into my pack and sigh happily. There is nothing quite like fresh air on my skin. The human females would squeal in distress at the sight of me, but they like to cover their bodies with furs. I think it is because they are always cold. To me, this weather is perfect.

I hop forward. "Come, Chahm-pee. Let us go see what our traps hold."

He bleats and moves to my side, keeping pace with me.

CHAHM-PEE GRAZES AS I WALK, nipping at tree bark and pulling at shoots as we move through the valleys and the steep cliffs. I see no one else out, but their tracks are everywhere. Not surprising—the hunters do not like to spend as long out on the trails as they used to, not now that so many of them have mates and small kits waiting for them to come home. It is the unmated hunters—myself included—who take the more distant trails. I do not mind; I like the exploring. Sometimes it feels like I am the only one out in the big wide world, and it is fascinating to me how empty and yet gorgeous my surroundings are.

I love this place.

I know the humans complain about the snow and the cold. I know there is more rock than they are used to, and No-rah has mentioned that their old home had many more trees. But when I look around, I see home. I see snow that hugs the world like a blanket. I see spikes of color where foliage has pushed its way through the snow, reaching for the sun. I see ribbons of blue as the streams wind through valleys, and herds of distant dvisti as they churn trails in the snow, seeking food. It is all fascinating and lovely and I could spend every day exploring and learning new things. Most of the humans are content to stay in the village. A few of them hunt, like Leezh and Li-lah and Mah-dee, but most are happy at home.

But I love the adventure of exploration. I crave new experiences. I want more than just sitting around a fire and chatting. I want to see everything I can.

As I walk, I contemplate this. *I want to get away for a few days,* I think. Let Sessah focus on something else for a change. But where? To the great salt lake, with its long scaly monsters that swim in it? To the human cave with the flashing red light that burns at a touch? Or somewhere else?

I think of Har-loh and what she would like. *She likes plants better than meat,* I think. Maybe…maybe I could visit Tee-fah-ni's fruit cave and bring her home a few things from there? It is not far from the Elders' Cave, and the grounds are familiar, if far away. It is a long journey, but I think of how Har-loh will smile at such a thing.

And I set off in that direction, Chahm-pee chewing as he moves beside me. He likes the fruit, too. And maybe when we are there, we can see if the Elders' cave is still tipped over.

All afternoon, I hike in that direction. The plants thin out atop the ridges, so I descend the cliffs and walk in the valleys with Chahm-pee. There are snow-cats around, and other dvisti herds, and I see the shadow of the occasional sky-claw, but they do not concern me. I am much larger than any of the small humans and it will not bother me, and Chahm-pee is far too fat to worry about the scrawny snow-cats. When the suns begin to move lower in the skies, I eat a few bites of the dried meat my mother sent along and contemplate where I shall sleep. There are two hunter caves close to me. One is but a short walk from here, but it is tiny and ill-suited for both sa-khui female and dvisti, and I will have to smell Chahm-pee make wind all night. Better to continue to the farther cave, which is larger...but it means journeying after dark.

I shrug off any concern. It is the bitter season, and I am strong. I have a knife and spear, and nothing should attack an adult sa-khui, especially not one accompanied by a large dvisti. It will be fine. But when I cross the next ridge, I see... something.

Something different.

At first I think it is my eyes playing tricks on me. A flash of light, and then it is gone. I squint up at the skies, my hand to my brow as I gaze at the clouds. Was it my imagination?

But then, there it is again. It flashes in the sky and then grows dark. It moves quickly, darting high up and between the clouds, moving like no bird or sky-claw I have ever seen before. I watch in wonder as it hovers over one of the distant cliffs, then zooms across the sky faster than I can follow. When the lights flash again, I realize what this is. It is another human cave, just like the one Shorshie and the others came from. We have visitors from the stars. For a moment, I am terrified. Maybe someone has come to take Shorshie and the other humans away? Back where they came from? But no, they have said many times that they did not come here willingly, and Kira made sure their cave did not go back to the skies.

These people are here for different reasons. They must be. But what?

CHAPTER 2

MARDOK

"I CAN'T BELIEVE WE GOTTA set down here. Do you know where the kef we are?" Trakan snarls, sticking another carcinogel between his lips and lighting it. His foot taps angrily on the floor of the main deck.

"You're the navigator," I tell him, keeping my tone slow and unconcerned as I scroll through screen after screen of error codes. "That's your job."

"Kopan Keffing VI," he snarls, and I can hear the angry smack of his fingers against his input station as he types. "Uninhabited keffing snowball of a planet, that's what it is."

"Better than Kopan V," Captain Chatav says, unruffled as he gazes out the monitors into space. "We'd be crispy if we landed any closer to that binary star. We're lucky to be this far out."

Trakan snorts and gets to his feet, storming off the bridge.

Chatav isn't concerned. He swigs his tea and regards the screen, lit up with engine diagnostics. Not much ruffles the captain. Not after serving half his life in the military and being shipped out to conflict after endless conflict. To him, this is probably cake and not an emergency. "You can fix this, Vendasi?"

"Probably," I tell him. "Might need to take the engine or the matter drive apart, but I'm positive I can at least patch us to the next spaceport if nothing else. And call me Mardok." Being called by my surname reminds me of my time in the military, and I'd rather not think about that shit. Not today. Not any day, really.

Today, though, I'm trying not to panic. I don't like that we're stuck here. I don't like being stranded. Not one keffing bit.

The captain nods at my response. "See to it then, Vendasi. I'll be in my quarters if you need me."

I don't correct him again. Been working with the captain for three years now and he still calls me Vendasi. Guess you can't take the military out of him, even after all this time. It's a game between us, one that's been going on for a long time. I tell him what to call me, and he calls me whatever the kef he pleases, because he's the captain. Most days I find it amusing. Today, it just irritates me. But I suck it up and do my best to not let it eat at me. Been down that road too many times. Let the small things get to me and I'll never get my head calm.

So I nod at the captain and grab my diagnostic pad. Everyone else gets to relax while we wait, but I get to work. Lucky me. I click a button on my console and lean in to give the order. "Computer, initiate landing."

IT'S NOT THE MATTER DRIVE. I figure that out about three hours into the diagnostic. That's a good thing, because if the matter drive is busted, we're straight up keffed. So if it isn't the matter drive, has to be the engine. The good news is that

I can likely fix the engine. The bad news is that I have to take it apart to see which parts are failing, and that means going outside onto Kopan VI.

In a way, I'm kind of looking forward to it. Spent the last few weeks on a medic station before returning to *The Tranquil Lady*, and before that, spent the last few years in space. Spent most of my time back in the military riding shuttles and at base stations, with a few ugly exceptions. Getting out in the open sounds kinda nice. According to my info-feed, the atmosphere's breathable. There are a few bad elements that need to be filtered out, so I clip an air-gen to my nose and wait for it to kick in. Once it does, I breathe deep. Amazing how something so small can even cut away the dank, metallic smell of the ship. I suck in another breath or two, then grab my di-pad and my tools, and hit the button for the hatch.

It creaks open, ice cracking off and falling away as the hatch door slides back. A blast of frigid air hits me in the face, and I immediately shut the hatch again with a slap of my hand over the button.

Kef. That is *cold* outside. I'm shocked that my regulating jumpsuit isn't able to handle the temperature. Feels colder than deep space, though I'm not sure that's possible.

I swallow the uneasiness I feel. *We're not stranded*, I remind myself. *It's an easy fix. The ship isn't critical, just has a minor problem. You can fix this.* I retreat backward into the ship, flexing my artificial arm. The metal can handle extreme temperatures, but it still feels colder than the rest of my body. I clench my fist over and over again, expecting to hear a creak in the metallic joints, but there is nothing. There never is. Flexing my hand, I head over to the gear station in the bay and suit up against the environment. I leave off a helmet— it's not necessary and I like for my eyes to be unobstructed

while I work. Niri has a scarf left in here, since she claims her
neck gets cold in enviro-suits. I wrap it around my exposed
neck, ignoring the fact that it's bright pink and yellow. It's
warm, and that's all that matters. Once I'm dressed, I slap
the door hatch again and close my eyes, bracing against the
bone-jarring cold. Guess I don't have to wonder about why
this place isn't inhabited. Not only is it in the middle of keffing nowhere, but it's also so cold it makes your cock freeze off.
I hunch against the brutal wind and head out, tools in hand.

On the underside of *The Tranquil Lady*, I'm mostly protected from the wind, and the cold isn't so bad. I unscrew
panels on the hull, setting them down carefully in the thick
snow before moving on to the next one. My diagnostic pad is
telling me that everything in the engine is working just fine,
which means that it's wrong and I'm going to have to pull
things apart and examine them, one by one, to determine
what the problem is. I don't mind working with my hands.
Calms the roar in my brain. Just wish it wasn't so cold. I get to
work, carefully removing one part and setting it down, then
another. A few of them are corroded in spots, which points to
a leak somewhere. Maybe there's not enough damage—yet—
to cause things to stop working completely, but enough to
cause the jerking in the accelerator, which is what concerned
Trakan and the captain in the first place. I forget all about the
cold after a few minutes of work, more interested in finding
the problem and determining the extent of the damage.

"Holy kef, it's colder than a tranki whore's tits out here."

Niri. I sigh inwardly. Gods love the old woman. She won't
leave me alone. Ever since I returned from my father's funeral,
she's been hovering like she's a mama zenda and I'm her spin-
dly legged colt. "Under here," I call out, because she's going to
find me anyhow. "Watch where you step."

"All this snow," Niri exclaims, and I hear her feet crunch on the ice. "Brr! Give me a regulated-temperature cabin any day of the week." As I glance over, she picks her way across the parts-strewn snow under the ship and makes her way toward me. She has a sweater held tightly around her lanky frame, and the metal tips on her horns are icing up. I imagine mine must be coated, too. She's got a breather on, at least.

"You're not dressed to be out here," I tell her, turning back to the next screw I'm carefully pulling out. It's corroded as well, and looking a bit stripped. Damn. Captain's going to blame me if this shit's all rundown and busted. It's my job to keep things in shape down here, and I'm wondering if I somehow missed something or if I've been too occupied to notice the poor state of the engine. Either way, I'm keffing ashamed.

"I won't be out here long. I just came out to see how you're doing." She comes and stands next to me, shivering as she gazes around her. "How's it look?"

"Not good."

"That's because you're a pessimist," she says crisply. "I'm sure you can fix it."

I'm sure I can, too. "Eventually. There's a leak in here somewhere. Hate that I missed something vital."

She makes a noise of agreement. "It's not like you to be sloppy, but you've had a lot on your mind."

Here we go. I remain silent, focused on my task so I don't have to think about what's coming up.

"How are you handling things? You've been quiet today. Not that you were very talky before, but I'm a woman. I notice these things."

Niri's also old enough to be my grandmother, and twice as nosy. "Fine."

She snorts, and I feel her thwack me on the side a moment later. "Don't give me that shit. Before you left you were all wounded inside and strong outside. Since you came back, you're just hollow all over. You wanna talk about it? Or about what's bothering you today?"

"No."

"Mardok, don't be an asshole."

I'm not. "That's Trakan's job. As for what's crawled up my ass…I just don't wanna be stranded." Understatement.

"Fair enough. And Trakan's an asshole because he's got a girl back at spaceport and misses her."

Does he? I didn't know. I wonder if I should feel guilty. We're a small crew—four strong—and we should be close. I should know if Trakan's got a girl waiting for him. I did notice he's been huffing carcinogels a lot more. "Mm."

"You got someone waiting back at spaceport for you?"

"No one."

"Well, that's your problem." Her crackling, imperious voice softens. "You're lonely."

I clench my jaw. I'm not lonely. Can't be lonely when you crew on a ship as small as this one. Can't afford it. I've been out on runs for months at a time. Never know when I'm going to be back somewhere for longer than a day or two, and that suits me fine. Haven't been with a girl since I left the military. Prefer it that way, really. No one to make miserable while I'm gone. No one to stay up at night, terrified and weeping and wondering if I'm missing in action, like my mother worried about my father. I've got my hand when I'm lonely enough. It'll do. "I'm fine."

"Was the funeral nice? Did they shoot the coffin into space, or did you buy a plot on one of the moons?"

Gods, she's not going away, is she? I bite back my sigh. "Cremated."

"Ah. And your family?"

"I'm it."

Her voice softens. "Are you sure you're all right, Mardok? I think of you like one of my sons, and you just don't seem to be yourself lately. I worry, that's all. Got nothing to do but look after you and Trakan on these long voyages. Captain Chatav's so healthy he doesn't even need a damn medic."

I grunt. She's not wrong. Chatav's very into balanced nutrition bars instead of meals, and drinks nothing but herbal teas. Works out every day in the ship gym and can probably bench press my entire body without breaking a sweat. Trakan's skinny and thin. I'm muscled, but I don't bulk. It'd look ridiculous with my bionic arm. As if my missing arm knows I'm thinking about it, it aches, and I flex my hand. Even with a metal arm and six years of living with it under my belt, the phantom pain doesn't go away. Probably never will. "Promise I'm fine."

I don't know what to say to her. The words stick in my throat. What do I tell someone like Niri, who's acerbic and cusses like any soldier but has the heart of the softest kitten? She'd never understand my relationship with my father. That we fell apart when my mother died and our last conversations together were angry, bitter ones. That I got the call two days after he died, and we never had final words to say to each other. That our last ones were full of hatred. That he thought I was a weakling for leaving the military behind, even after it shattered my body and nearly broke my mind. I still dream about the people on Uzocar IV, and my men. I still hear them screaming. In my mind, I still hear the ship flying away…without us on it. Sometimes when I close my eyes, I can smell the bodies of the dead. It still kefs with my sleep.

My father's funeral was a military one. Being there around all those soldiers? Brought back all the hell I've worked for six years to bury. Made me remember, when I took a job on

The Tranquil Lady specifically to forget. Which reminds me. "You still got the sleep meds I like, Niri?"

"I do." The concern creeps back into her voice. "You're not sleeping again?"

"Not enough." I want to leave it at that, but my artificial arm cramps up with another phantom pain and I nearly drop the wrench I'm holding. I pull away from the half-dismantled engine and glance over at her. There's concern written all over her pale blue face, almost comical given the amount of ice forming on the decorative metal capping her horns. "Just tired," I add, and rub my face with my good hand. "Sometimes I'm not sure what I'm doing here. Captain deserves a better mech."

"You know this crew. We hire people that don't ask questions." She reaches out and pats my arm. "Besides, you're so big that you're security as well as mech. Two for one. You know Chatav's a cheap bastard."

I snort. That he is. "Go inside, Niri. I'm fine, I promise. We'll talk later."

She nods and pulls her thin sweater tighter around her frame. "I'll get those meds for you and we'll chat. Dinner?"

"Dinner's good. Thanks." It'll make her feel better to mother me for a few hours.

Niri gives me a faint smile and heads back inside, her tail flicking in the wind.

I'm alone again with my thoughts and the snow. I watch her leave, contemplating. Maybe she's right and I've been more silent than usual, sloppier on the job. I don't mind being a mech. I don't even mind being security. Ever since my father's death, though…I'm just tired. Hollowed out. Like nothing's left of me after the war on Rede System IV. Thought I'd gotten better at handling it, but after the funeral, I think I realized I haven't been handling it at all. I've just buried it, and seeing my father—my angry, proud, bitter father—put into a coffin pushed me right back over the edge again.

I sigh to myself and return to my work, tugging at a loose screw. Shouldn't matter that I'm nothing but broken parts inside. That's why people crew on long-distance freighters like *The Tranquil Lady*. Got nothing going on in their lives. I go back to work, filling my mind with the problem at hand and not problems long gone. Don't want that shit in my head.

I don't know how long I'm working after that. I lose myself in the gears that fit together, the small, intricate parts that play such a vital role in the complex engine of the ship. It's like a puzzle, and I enjoy figuring out which pieces are needing attention. I'm lost in thought, my hands around an oily gear, when I hear a sound behind me. It's a gasp, small and feminine. Niri. I pull my filthy hands free and glance over my shoulder.

It's not Niri.

It's…a woman. A stranger.

I must be hallucinating, because she's gorgeous. Something out of a dream with arching, proud horns, long black hair, and a hauntingly lovely face. Her eyes glow a strange, bright blue, and she's completely, utterly keffing naked except for the tiniest of loincloths.

That does it. I've lost it. I've finally snapped.

She beams at me, all white teeth and vibrant blue skin, her tail fluttering back and forth with interest. She looks at me with awe and wonder both on her face, and she's…just breathtakingly beautiful. I'm stunned by how perfect she is, from the high, tight buds of her breasts to the long, muscular length of her legs. I don't know how she's not freezing out here, because she's wearing absolutely nothing.

Of course, she's imaginary, so I don't suppose it matters.

She says something, her glowing eyes distracting me, and

she picks up one of the discarded parts. She cocks her head at me like she's just asked a question.

"Sweetheart, if you're a dream of mine, you'd be less interested in the mechanical parts and more interested in mine," I murmur. Even though I haven't felt the need for female companionship in a long, long keffing time, the sight of this woman is making my cock stir uncomfortably. It has to be because she's so naked and so...fit and lean. There's not an ounce of fat on her body. Her perfect, perfect body.

The girl says something again and holds the gear out to me. Her long hair blows in the wind, and I see she has a few braids tangled in with the long, glossy locks. Her horns aren't capped and she's got no tattoos, no body art whatsoever. She looks wild and primitive, and...and I must be completely crazy, because she looks so keffing real and utterly sexy.

But this planet is deserted. Inhospitable. The air has traces of poison in it. "You're *not* real, are you?"

Her brows pinch, and her mouth turns down. She gestures at the gear again, her gaze flicking over me with avid curiosity. I notice she keeps stopping at my horns and my facial tattoos. I have a feeling that if my bionic arm were uncovered, she'd stare at that, too. Normally it bugs me when people stare, but I don't think there's malice or glee in this imaginary woman, just curiosity. Curiosity and sheer, abandoned beauty.

I guess my spank material is taking a turn toward the odd. Huh. I take the gear from her hands, and as I do, our fingers brush.

And that's when I realize three things.

She's real, she's incredibly warm, and she's purring.

FARLI

I watch the cave land in the distance, fascinated. It settles down like a lumbering sa-kohtsk, blowing snow in every direction and making my hair whip wildly about my head as if there's an incredibly strong storm. The skies are clear, though, so the wind must be coming from the cave. How curious. Something high-pitched whines and roars as it descends, loud enough to frighten Chahm-pee back over the ridge. I know he will return, so I do not chase after him. He knows he is safe with me.

I am not frightened, not yet. I want to see what these people are doing, and why they are landing their cave here. If I see they are the bad ones with the orange skin like the others mentioned, then I will run away and tell the chief. Until then, I admire the beauty and the strangeness of their flying cave. How can something so square and fat move through the skies like a bird? It does not seem possible.

It is on the ground, quiet, for a long time before one of the sides opens an eye. No, I decide a moment later. It is not an eye, but opening an entryway. A male steps out. At least, I think it's a male. And what I see makes me suck in a breath.

His body is covered by some strange, thick gray leather, but he is tall, so tall. Taller than anyone in the tribe, even Raahosh. His head is exposed, and I can see he has blue skin, like mine, but paler. He also has a sweep of arching, proud horns that gleam in the sunlight. Strange. His mane is shorn close to his scalp, but it looks to be black, like mine.

This tall stranger is sa-khui. He is not the orange-skinned bad ones like Shorshie and the others mentioned. He is one of our people. I bet he is handsome, too. I cannot tell from here, but I like the way he moves.

A stranger.

A handsome stranger.

I am so excited at this that I climb over the hill and begin to approach. I want to say hello, to greet him, to ask him why his horns are shiny and where his mane went. To ask him why he is pulling the guts out of the cave and spreading them on the snow. Before I can take more than a step, the archway on the side of the cave opens again, and this time a female steps out. I frown to myself and duck back behind the rocks. Is this his mate?

The male stops pulling the guts out and pauses to talk to the female. I study them and determine this must be his mother, not his mate. She is much older, and his manner reminds me of my brothers with my mother—affectionate but impatient. I am curiously relieved, and watch as they continue to talk. My gaze always strays back to the male. From this distance I cannot make out his features, but I like the way he moves, strong and sure. My heart flutters in my chest when he flicks his tail and turns his back on the female, returning to his project. He pulls a few more parts out, and the female returns to the ship, shivering like the humans do, even on a pleasant day. I wait for her to leave, and then when I know the male is alone, I emerge from my hiding spot.

I am excited to talk to him. I have so many questions to ask. Did he come here with humans? Is he bringing mates to the others? Is he...looking for a mate? The thought makes my entire body flush with excitement. I pick my steps carefully in the snow, moving silently as any good hunter does.

As I venture closer, I get a better look at his face. He is turned to the side, but I can see that he has proud features and a noble nose. He is handsome, too, just like I knew he would be, and the line of his jaw is proud and unyielding. His eyes are shielded by heavy brows, and plated like my own. I cannot get over how different—but similar—he is to the males in my tribe. He is so like us, and yet...so much handsomer. I could stare at this appealing face for days and never grow bored. The differences are fascinating—like his tail. He has a tail, but for some reason it is blunted, half the length of my own. Has it always been like that, or did he lose it in an accident? His horns with the strange shiny tips fascinate me, as does the fact that his mane is gone. I can see dark stubble on his scalp, and it highlights the strong lines of his skull. Fascinating. He turns to the side, studying one of the parts he has pulled from the underbelly of the cave, and I realize that the dark shadows I thought were from the ship are something else entirely. He has...designs on his face. Celebration designs, like the ones I paint on the others when we have a feast. One entire side of his face is marked with them.

I gasp at the sight, because it is beautiful and surprising all at once. Is he celebrating something today?

He straightens, turning toward me. His eyes go wide at the sight of me, and he looks me up and down, as if unable to believe that I am here.

"Greetings to you," I call out.

"Kzzv si metalsivak?"

His eyes are dark, I realize. There is no glow of a khui inside them. It is like when the humans first arrived and their eyes were dead. Creepy. I hold back a shiver.

He stares at me expectantly. I do not know his words, and the way he watches me fills me with a new feeling—worry. Is...is he not here to visit, then? I feel shy under the weight of his gaze, which is strange. I am not normally flustered, but this is also the first time I have ever talked to a male not in my tribe. I pick up one of the pieces of the cave and hold it out to him. "Do you need this?"

He squints, and it is clear he does not understand my words. His gaze moves over my body again, and I feel a tingle of excitement and pleasure as he studies me. He is looking at me like the other males regard their mates. It makes my nipples tighten with excitement, and I feel a warm pulsing between my thighs. He looks at me the way I want to be looked at by a male, I realize. Not like Sessah with his silly devotion, or Taushen with his impatient courting. He devours me with his eyes and I…I like it.

The male says something again, and I frown, because I want to understand his words. I offer him the cave part I hold in my hand, curious if that is what he wants. As I get nearer to him, I start to tremble in my belly. It's strange, because I do not feel fear. If anything, I am excited and aroused by the sight of this male. I take another step closer to him…and then it hits me.

Resonance.

The tremble in my belly is not trembling, after all.

It is my khui, singing with such force that it is making my entire body shake. The song rises in my throat, and I stare at this male in wonder. This stranger, this handsome hunter with paint on his face and strange shiny horns is to be my mate. We will make kits together and he will hold me in his arms and we will be a family.

I am so happy.

"My mate," I say with joy, and extend my hands to him. He does not move forward, but he takes the cave part from my hand, and our fingers brush. My pulse thrums with delight at that small touch, and I feel a growing slickness between my thighs. I want him. I am ready to mate, right here and right now.

He gazes at my hand in wonder, where our fingers touch. Surely he feels the same thing I do. "My mate," I say again, and put my hands on his face. He stares at me with wide eyes. He is shocked, I imagine, but I will be a good mate to him. I lean forward and press my mouth to his in the human mouth-matings that the others make look so very pleasurable. His lips are cooler under mine. His skin, too. Is he cold? He will warm up when he takes his khui.

The male jerks backward, away from my touch.

"It is all right," I tell him, excited. "It is a human gesture, nothing more."

He says something again, and his gloved hand goes to his mouth. He touches his lips, then glances over at the cave, where the entrance opened. He speaks, spitting out a string of fluid-sounding words.

"I do not understand your language," I say, fretting. We no longer have the Elders' Cave to teach languages. It is on its side. "Perhaps you have something in your cave that can teach you to speak with me?" Now that I am standing so close to him, I want to pull off the strange leather tunic he wears that covers him from boot to neck. He has a bit of colorful leather tucked around his throat, and I can see it move as he swallows hard, then slurs another round of gibberish at me.

He rubs his arms and repeats one word, gazing at me. "Fasang?" Oh. My mate is trying to communicate. I smile at him and listen patiently, but I am more fascinated by the dancing lines that cover one side of his face. They have not moved, and they did not feel wet when I touched them. It is almost as if they are permanently on the skin. Would that not be fascinating? I wonder how he did it, and how he got his horns so shiny and silver. He rubs his arms again and repeats the word. "Fasang?"

Is he asking if I am cold? I laugh, because the idea is so funny. "Why would I be cold? Today is a perfect day."

His expression changes. The frustration fades from his face, and a hint of a smile tugs at the corners of his hard mouth. "Fasang la?" He rubs his arms again and then touches my arm with a small shake of his head.

I decide that I love his smile. It seems so hesitant, and I want to make him smile more. Actually, I want to press my mouth to his again and try more mouth-mating. "Do you want to mate here, or do you want to go back to my cave?" I gesture at the distant hills. There is a hunter cave nearby, full of furs and supplies. "We will be alone there."

"Fasang la?"

Are we still on that? I want to see him smile again. I want his touch. So I take his hand in mine, and note the strange glove he wears. It feels like thin, slippery leather. I tug at it to remove the glove.

He jerks his hand away.

I draw back, wounded. "What did I do?"

He shakes his head and says something new, something different, and then offers me his other hand. Strange. I touch the glove again, and he nods, indicating I can continue. All right. I pull the glove off and notice his strange markings on his face continue onto his skin here. "So beautiful," I breathe, tracing the whorls and dark lines. "What does it mean?"

He says nothing, and I wish we understood each other better. I will just have to learn patience. I cannot wait to hear all the exciting things he will tell me.

He is not pulling his hand out of my grip this time, though, and I smile at him, stroking his palm. It is hard and callused, like that of any hunter. He does not feel as warm as I do, but I do not mind. He is mine. I take his hand and place it on my teat. "Mate? I am ready."

I feel his shock ripple through his body. His mouth opens slightly, and he stares at me in surprise, but he does not remove his hand. My khui sings so loudly between us, and I am practically throbbing with the song of it. I am nervous, too. Will he take me up on my offer, or will he fight against it, like Jo-see did to Haeden? I ache to feel his big hands everywhere. I want everything he has to offer me, and more. His voice is very soft when he speaks again, and he pulls his hand slowly away. "Na mahas tikla qi tqand."

I do not know his words, but when he puts his glove back on, it feels like rejection. Hot tears flood my eyes. "Do you… not like me?" How can my mate reject me so quickly? Is there something wrong?

The stranger shakes his head, saying more of the jarring words, and brushes the tears off my cheek before they can freeze. His touch is instantly comforting, and I want to burrow against him and feel what it would be like for his arms to go around me. I always wondered what it would be like to resonate to someone, but I never imagined it to be this overwhelming this fast.

A familiar bleat sounds in the distance. Chahm-pee is returning. I pull away from the stranger and turn around. My fat dvisti stands a short distance away, galloping forward and spraying snow in that funny, kit-like, eager way he does to make me laugh.

My mate grabs me by the arm, shoving me behind him, and bellows out a word. "Skavash!"

"It is my pet," I tell him, patting his shoulder even as he pulls something from his belt.

I do not know what he's doing until his hand moves, and then there's a sizzling sound. Something flashes. Chahm-pee gives a cry of pain and collapses to the ground.

"No! Chahm-pee!" I scream, rushing forward. The male tries to hold me back, but I shove his arms away and rush forward to my pet. My poor, sweet Chahm-pee. All he wanted to do was greet me. I drop to my knees at his side. He is wheezing, blood spilling into the snow. The smell of charred fur and cooked meat makes me want to vomit, as does the look of pain and fear in his liquid blue eyes. I stroke his nose gently. "It is going to be all right," I whisper to him. "I am here."

CHAPTER 3

MARDOK

GODS DAMN IT, I THINK I just shot her keffing pet.

I put my blaster away, tucking it back into its holster as the strange, nearly naked woman sobs over the furry herbivore. I'm disgusted that I overreacted. Now that I have a moment to catch my breath, I realize that the thing is a four-legged plant eater, shaggy, ugly, but harmless. I just saw it charging toward us and reacted like a soldier.

But I'm not a soldier any longer, and I keffed up. Bad.

The woman sobs over her pet, stroking its nose as the creature wheezes its final breaths. There's blood everywhere, and I have the awful, terrible sensation that I've messed this up, bad. I shouldn't have shot first. This strange, wild girl clearly loves her animal, and she wanted to be my friend.

I think of the look on her face as she put my hand on her breast, full of need and longing. Yeah, she wanted to be a lot more than friends. And now my cock hurts in my pants, and my heart hurts because I just murdered something she loved out of a knee-jerk reaction. I need to fix this, but how? I move closer, edging forward. The creature isn't getting up. His head is in her lap, and he breathes shallowly, making little sounds of pain as she cries over him. He's been gut-shot, and while he's bleeding a lot, he's not exactly dying fast.

Keffing awful.

If it was just me and he was an enemy soldier, I'd give him a second blast to the head to ease his suffering. But I don't think the strange, beautiful female would like that. Not in the slightest. So…what?

I'm full of remorse. Not that I shot the creature—because any soldier wouldn't hesitate to take down a charging animal—but that it clearly means something to her and I've destroyed that. She tosses a look in my direction, and her face is wet with tears. She spits words at me, and I don't have to speak her language to know what she's saying.

How could you?

I rub a hand over the bristle on my skull. All right, what now? Wait for it to die? Put it out of its misery? I think of the way she smiled at me, putting my hand on her breast, the trust and happiness in her face. I haven't seen that in…kef, who knows how long.

And I want it back. I feel a violent surge of possessiveness toward the woman. I saw her first. She's mine. I think of Trakan heading out of the ship to smoke one of his carcinogels. Would she approach him with her smiles and nakedness? Put his hand on her breast and invite him with her eyes? I clench my hands so tight I can almost hear the metal creak in my bionic arm.

All right. If she's mine, then I need to fix this. I slap my communicator on my wrist, turning it on, and lift it to my mouth. "Niri, head to med bay, would you? I'm coming in and you're needed."

She immediately clicks back. "Are you all right? Did you hurt yourself?"

"Just go to med bay," I tell her, and move forward. I head to the other side of the smelly, furry creature and heft him into my arms. He's enormous and probably weighs twice what I do, with long, dangling legs and so much fur that I'm going to be pulling it out of my molars for weeks to come. But he's not fighting me, and his head is limp. I tilt so the majority of his weight falls on my bionic arm, and then stagger toward the entrance of the ship.

The woman follows after me. I almost expect her to shout in her angry, babbling language, or to hit me with those delicate hands of hers, but she doesn't. She hovers at my heels, her sniffs the only sounds she makes. The hatch opens automatically, and I head inside, turning sideways to go through the narrow entrance. The creature's bleeding all over me and all over the floors, but right now that doesn't matter. What matters is making sure it doesn't die, because I don't think I'll be able to stand it if this strange woman looks at me with hate…or worse, disappointment. Hate can always be flipped back to friendship, but disappointment lasts forever.

"What is going on?" Niri calls as she enters the ship's main narrow passageway. She gasps, flattening herself against the wall as she sees me with the furry, bleeding monstrosity. "What the kef is that thing?"

"This planet?" I growl. "It's not uninhabited."

"Is that one of the locals?" Niri asks, her eyes wide as she hurries back toward med bay. Inside, I can hear the hum of her computers as they power up. "Did he talk to you?"

"No. It's complicated."

"I see. I don't know if he's going to fit on the diagnostic bed." She moves to the control panel and taps a few buttons, and the metal bed rolls out of the compartment with a soft hiss.

I heft my burden onto it and stagger backward the moment he's out of my arms. Gods, that thing was heavy. I glance down at my enviro-suit and it's covered in blood. I unzip it and begin to unbuckle my way out of the cumbersome thing. Niri busies herself with the creature. When the legs don't tuck into the bed itself, she gives up on sending it through the diagnostic scanner and takes out a handheld, moving it over the creature.

"I can tell you what's wrong," I say gruffly as I pry the insulated boots off my feet. "I keffing shot him. He was charging at us."

"Us?" Niri turns and frowns at me. "What are you talking about?"

"The girl." Her brows go up, and I turn, realizing that my new friend didn't follow me into the med clinic. "Shit. Be right back." I shove the filthy enviro-suit aside and race back into the hall, looking for her. If Trakan sees her…

But there she is, standing near the doorway that leads to the bridge. She's admiring one of the wall panels, touching a light as it flashes up on screen. It's a weather reading of the outdoors, and I'm pretty sure she can't read what it says, but she seems fascinated by it. I move to her side, and she jerks in surprise at the sight of me. Must not hate me too much, though, because she immediately starts purring again, and that makes me feel better.

"Tisik," she says, pointing at the screen. "Vo?"

I have no clue what she's saying. "Do you like the lights? Or do you want to know what it says?"

She sighs heavily and gives her head a little shake. "Ne vo." She gazes at me, frowning as she studies my chest. I rub a hand over it, wondering if there's something wrong with my crew jumpsuit. It ain't much to look at, but considering I spend ninety-nine percent of my days in space with only three other people, I don't much care what I look like. And it's not like a naked chick's gonna be a fashion critic, right?

She pats my chest, and then looks up at me, frowning. "Are you wondering where my clothes went? They're still here. Speaking of..." I untuck my shirt and pull it over my head, then offer it to her.

She takes it and raises it to her nose, gently sniffing it. After a moment, she pets the fabric and gives me another curious glance. Her fingers reach out and she touches my chest, the scars over my heart-plating, and the line where my flesh meets the bionic arm. It's making my body respond, and I need to shut this shit down fast before I remember that it's been well over three years since I slept with a woman. I take the shirt and pull it over her shoulders, then help her work her arm through the sleeve. She giggles, the sound light and achingly sweet, as I button her into it.

Once I'm done dressing her like a toddler, she's, well, she's covered at least. My shirt hangs off her like a tent, but at least she's no longer naked. I'd say I'm glad she's warm, but I don't think cold has been a problem for her, period.

Her hand touches my arm, her fingers stroking my skin. "Chahm-pee?" She wiggles her nose and then mimes galloping with her hands.

"Is that your pet? Come on. I'll take you to him." I clasp her hand in mine, and she squeezes my fingers. Hate that she feels so keffing right with her little fingers tucked against mine.

I lead her to med bay, and she sucks in a breath at the sight of her animal laid out. Niri's put away her diagnostic machine and has a screen in front of her face, directing the surgery manually. "You blew a hole right through his keffing guts, dumbass," Niri tells me as I return. "Lucky for you I could remove the part of the liver that you blew up without him going toxic, though it's tricky given that he's an animal and our machines aren't prepped to—" Her words trail off as she sees the girl with me. "Who the kef is that?"

"I don't know," I say bluntly. "She came up to me outside."

Niri studies her, then sets the machine on automatic as it works at stitching up the wound in the unconscious hairball of a creature. "She's wearing your shirt. She naked under that?"

"Loincloth."

"In this snow? Is she crazy?"

"I…think she lives here." Something tells me she's not crazy, just…wild. "Didn't Trakan say this place was uninhabited?"

"According to planetary surveys, yeah. You think she's a shipwreck survivor? She looks like us. Clearly mesakkah."

"Sa-khui," the girl chimes in, misinterpreting Niri's words. She taps her chest. "Sa-khui."

"Is that your name, sweetie?" Niri asks, pulling the girl away from me and moving her to a seat. She takes out her hand scanner and begins to run it over her.

"Sa-khui," the girl repeats again, and taps her chest. Then she pats Niri's arm. "Sa-khui." She gestures toward me. "Sa-khui?"

"I think she's saying she's like us," I tell Niri, leaning against the wall and crossing my arms over my chest. Smart thing. I can't deny that I'm attracted to her like mad, but wouldn't any man in my situation? Long time celibate, naked, attractive girl…but there's something more to her. Maybe it's her sweet, innocent expression, her wide-eyed wonder as she looks around her. Makes me want to protect her from anything that might harm her…even me. Or Niri. The captain. Trakan.

Not that I think they would… It's just that she's mine.

"Well, she's definitely descended from mesakkah stock,"

Niri says, interrupting my possessive thoughts. "The scan reads that her DNA matches up perfectly with ours. But she's not speaking any tongue that I know of."

"She stranded here, then?"

"I don't know. I think she was born on this planet." Niri moves the scanner over her. "I don't see any signs of tech implants anywhere. No surgical scars, no dental modifications, nothing. She doesn't have a single vaccine, and she's got parasites. Isn't that grand?"

"But she's healthy?"

"Oh, she's stunningly healthy," Niri says, putting her scanner away with a click. "Other than the parasites, of course. I can remove them once we're done with her pet here."

"And the eyes?"

She shrugs, putting her equipment away and checking on the herbivore. "Possibly a chemical reaction to something she ate? I don't know. Like I said, everything registers as healthy."

"Sa-khui?" the girl says again, looking over at me. "Vo?"

She wants answers, and I don't blame her. I tap my chest. "Mesakkah. That's my people. I'm from Ubeduc VII, Cap City." I point at Niri. "She's mesakkah, too, but she's from the homeworld, Kes. And that's probably way more than you needed to know."

"Cap see-tee?" she replies, tilting her head. She gestures at me. "Cap see-tee?"

"I think she thinks it's your name," Niri murmurs, amused. "I need to work on her furry little friend here. You want to take her to your station and see if you can get a language scan to match?"

It's a brilliant idea, and I'm annoyed I didn't think of it. I've been scrambled ever since the girl ran right into my arms, buck naked. "Will do. Come on," I say to the strange woman, and offer her my hand.

She looks at her pet, worried. "Chahm-pee?"

"He's going to be fine," I tell her, keeping my tone reassuring. It must work, because she puts her hand in mine, and I lead her out of the room and onto the bridge. Luckily, the captain and Trakan both must be in their quarters, because it's deserted. I move to my seat and turn on my work station. I fire up a translator and make her sit down in my seat, then crouch next to her. "Need you to talk."

She touches my arm. "Cap see-tee?"

I sigh and rub my brows. Kef. She probably does think that's my name now. Nothing to be done about it until I figure out what language she's speaking and set my aural implants to the correct frequency. I gesture at my mouth. "Talk."

"Spisak?" She gives me a curious look.

All right, maybe I need to try a different tactic. "Cap City," I say again, and tap my chest, then I gesture at her. "You?"

Her smile broadens, and she's so stunningly gorgeous that it takes my breath away and makes my blood quicken. There's nothing coy about her smile; she just beams at me like she's the happiest person in the world, and I love it. She begins to chatter, gesturing at her chest and letting out a stream of words that are so quick that I can't follow them. If her name's in there, I've lost it.

The language program starts to run, scanning through all the sounds she's spitting out, and when I gesture for her to keep talking, she does. After a moment, the computer comes back with an answer.

88% match - Old Sakh.

Holy kef. Old Sakh? From the Old Sakh Empire? No one's spoken that language in a thousand years. The Sakh Empire broke up and formed several coalitions of different planets, and my home world is one of them. Niri's, too. Well, that explains why I can't make heads or tails of what she's saying.

I tap a few commands into the computer, sending the language file to my aural implants, and wait for it to start up. It chimes a moment later, letting me know the sync is complete, and I gesture for her to talk again.

She hesitates. "I am not sure what you wish me to speak about. I have already told you about my people and my home, but it is useless. You do not hear my words."

I can't help but grin. "I hear them now."

Her eyes go wide.

FARLI

HE FINALLY SPEAKS WORDS I know! I smother my gasp and reach for his grinning face, wanting to caress his mouth. "Say it again."

"I know your language now. Kind of an obscure one, but I have it." He reaches past me to peck at the strange table. "I'll send it to Niri's oh-rahl eem-plants, too, so she can talk with you."

"Niri. Is that the female?"

He nods at me. "That's her name. What's yours?"

Oh, he wants to know my name. I squirm in my seat, filled with joy and a touch of arousal. He's looking at me, so pleased, and it makes me feel all flushed inside...though that could be the temperature in their cave. It is uncomfortably hot in here. "I am called Farli."

"Farli," he repeats, and he says it strangely, clipping the sounds with his tongue. I do not even care; it sounds beautiful to my ears. "I like it. Pretty."

I brim with happiness. "I like your name, too, Cap see-tee."

He chuckles, and I feel as if he's touching my teats just with that delicious laugh. "Cap City isn't my name. That's where I come from. I'm sorry if it was confusing to you." He puts his hand on my knee, and I feel scorched from that small touch. "My full name is Bron Mardok Vendasi, but you can call me Mardok."

Such a strange name. So long and fluid. I am fascinated by this. Fascinated by *him*. "How did you learn my language so fast? Did your cave tell you?" I look around. "I do not see a red beam to shoot into your eye."

"Huh?"

"That is how we learned the human language. The Elders' Cave spoke, and we told it to teach us to communicate with them, and it gave us words." I tap my eye. "A red beam of light went right here and gave me language."

He rubs his ear. "Translation must be off, because none of that made any sense to me."

I am crushed. "I apologize."

"Nothing to apologize for, Farli." His thumb brushes over my knee, and I feel the liquid warmth sliding between my thighs. I am resonating so very hard right now, and it's distracting me. "You can call me Cap City if you want."

"I will call you by your name. Mardok." I do not say it exactly as he does, but he smiles anyhow, and I feel better.

"What are you doing here, Farli? Near the ship?"

Ship? "Is that what your cave is? A ship?" I look around in wonder. So it is not a cave, after all. Ship. I mentally store the word to share with my chief and the others when I return to the tribe. "And I am hunting with Chahm-pee." I bite my lip and look back at him, my tail flicking in agitation. "Will he be all right? I do not understand what happened."

He looks upset. "I jumped the gun. Made a mistake. Niri is working on him right now."

"She is your healer?" I do not understand everything he

said, but it can be told another time."

"Of a sort yes."

"Will he live?" I feel the tears approach again. "He is fearless because I have raised him since he was a kit. He does not know to be afraid of sa-khui. He does not think he is food. He is a pet."

Mardok looks even more pained at my words. "It's my fault. I'm going to make this right for you, I promise."

I do not understand how it is his fault. Did he make the flash attack Chahm-pee? "The healer will cure him," I reassure him, though I do not know if this is true. "All will be well."

He studies me. "I have a million things I want to ask you, Farli."

"And I, you. We are one." I wait for him to bring up our resonance, but when my khui sings louder to him and he remains silent, I realize…I am the only one resonating. It is like when Vektal met Shorshie and he told us that she did not resonate until she had a khui. Oh. I am disappointed to realize he does not feel what I do. Well, I must simply go back to the tribe and organize a hunting party to go after a sa-kohtsk so my mate can remain here with me. I have so many things I need to tell him, but when I look back at him and he is half-naked and his skin is covered with the strange, whirling designs, I am distracted by his nearness.

Some hunter I am. A handsome stranger walks in front of me and my mind turns to scrambled eggs, like the kind Staysee makes for breakfast.

"How did you get here? To this place? And aren't you cold?" He crouches near my feet, looking up at me expectantly.

"Cold? In here? I am sweating." I fan my face with my hand. It seems easier to blame my flustered, heated cheeks on the warm air than my own need. "It feels nice outside.

Good weather."

He looks surprised. "This is good weather?"

"In the brutal season, it is much, much worse. More snow. The air is so cold it hurts to breathe in." I shrug. "But then it warms all over again and the suns come out."

He shakes his head. "Kef me. That's incredible. And it doesn't bother you? The cold?"

"The khui keeps me warm." I tap my breast. "The humans were cold before they had theirs put in. You will be fine once you acquire one."

"A khui?" He repeats the word, though it is clear he does not know what it is.

"The creature in my chest," I tell him. "It keeps me healthy and strong. It protects me from getting sick. It makes the air safe to breathe. It picks the best mate for me so we will have strong kits."

He looks distracted, and it is clear to me he is not listening to my words. "A symbiont," he murmurs. "Does everyone on your world have these?"

"Every living thing. Even Chahm-pee has one. You can see it in the eyes," I tell him, gesturing at my face. "They are bright blue with life, not dead and lifeless." *Like yours.* I do not say it, because that would hurt his feelings. He cannot help it. He will have bright, healthy eyes once he has a khui in his chest.

"Blue eyes," he murmurs. "Well, that explains it. Come on. We need to tell Niri before she removes your friend's symbiont and does more damage than she thinks."

I put my hand in his again and let him lead me to the back of the cave-ship. Anywhere he wants to lead me, I will happily go.

* * *

CHAHM-PEE IS FINE, THOUGH I do not think Niri likes the idea of leaving the khui in his chest—or mine. Their reactions do not bother me; I am told Shorshie and the other humans had a similar reaction to the thought of having a khui, but now they are content and healthy. A khui is a good thing. Chahm-pee's wounds have been closed up and the blood wiped off his fur, but he is still very quiet and unmoving. I stroke his nose, worried. "He will be all right?"

"He just needs to sleep," Niri assures me. "We will keep him in med bay overnight, and he should be good to go by the morning."

Such a fast recovery for such a terrible wound. I am impressed. "You are a good healer, Niri."

"Mm. Can I talk to you for a minute, Mardok? In private?" She gives him a pointed look and steps to the far end of the room.

Mardok looks over at me, and then follows Niri. A moment later, they are talking in their strange language, the one I do not understand. Niri is clearly agitated, her tail flicking as she talks. Mardok does not seem happy either, but his body remains still and attentive, like a hunter waiting on prey. I can hear them speak, even if I cannot make out the words, and I am sure they are talking about me. They do not like that I am here, for whatever reason. Perhaps they worry about their safety? I know my chief would be concerned to hear another cave-ship has landed, even if it is one full of friends and not enemies.

Mardok's answers to Niri are very short and blunt. He is not a talker, my mate. I do not mind that. He seems like Asha—someone with hurts buried deep. It makes me ache for him, because he is my mate and I want to help. Perhaps the love I have for him and the kit we make together will carry the pain out of his eyes, like it did for Asha and Hemalo.

I like the thought very much.

They both look over at me. "She should meet the captain," Niri says with a smile that does not reach her eyes. "Did you send him the language file?"

My mate sighs heavily. "I guess I should. I can't put it off, can I?"

I do not understand why they both look so unhappy.

MARDOK

THE CAPTAIN ISN'T PLEASED. THE captain isn't even remotely pleased. I explain to him the situation with Farli, and the fact that there are more people—more mesakkah, no less—living somewhere on this snowball of a planet, and marooned.

"Old Sakh?" He looks thoughtful as he swirls his tea in his favorite mug. "Ancient history. How did they get here?"

"The Sakh Empire was space-faring," I remind him. "The technology wasn't what we have, of course, but they were still very capable." I glance back at Farli, who is sitting in the ship's mess hall with Niri. The medic's been told to keep her busy while I explain things to the captain, and right now Niri is showing Farli how to brew tea through the computer system. I can only imagine the wonder and delight in Farli's mind as she pushes buttons and makes tea come out, and I hate that I'm not there at her side.

"And you're sure this isn't a plant of some kind? That she's not a spy?"

I look at him like he's crazy. "Captain, this is a remote snowball not even near any shipping lanes or disputed territory. What would she spy on?"

"Us?"

All that military background finally made the man's mind snap, I decide. "We're a long-haul freighter. Right now we're carrying kelp from Eldirav V." It's a high-end product, but it isn't exactly worth spying over. "Can't say that there's a need to spy on greens."

The captain grunts, like he doesn't quite believe me but doesn't have any other theories, either. "I find it hard to believe she knows nothing about us. Or the ship."

I'm pretty sure she knows nothing about nothing. Farli's a blank slate when it comes to our world. In a way, it's kind of charming. It's also utterly terrifying because it makes her helpless. I still don't think she realizes I shot her pet. I don't think she has any idea of what a blaster is.

I envy her that.

The captain doesn't look convinced. "So she's just lost, then?"

I bite back my sigh. The captain's a good man, but stubborn. "Don't think she sees it that way. This is her home. I don't think she's ever known anything but this place, not if she's speaking Old Sakh."

"How many of her people are here?"

I shrug. "Your guess is as good as mine. She hasn't said much about them, but I don't think she's hiding anything." I feel strangely protective of her, and I don't like that the captain's being a pain in the ass about her. She means no harm. If anything, we're the harmful ones. I've known her for all of an hour or two and I already tried to kill her damn pet.

Chatav considers this carefully, then nods. "I'll determine what to do with her over dinner. Be sure she's dressed appropriately." He turns his back to me and marches out of med bay, military-crisp.

Keffing hell. Dinner? Every time the ship has visitors, the captain loves to put on a military-style formal dinner for everyone. It's more or less the politest interrogation possible. I was hoping he wouldn't pull this shit, but the captain loves ceremony. "I don't know if it's a good idea for Trakan to know that she's here," I call after the captain's back.

"I did not ask you, Vendasi." The captain's response is icy. He doesn't even turn around. "This is a small crew. We don't keep secrets from each other."

Sure we don't. We just don't ask about shit we don't want to know about. I rub my jaw. "Fine."

I don't like this, but I don't have a choice. I'm not in charge here, and even if I dig my heels in, Niri and Trakan will go with what the captain says. I'm just the mech. But I can't get over the feeling that I'm somehow ruining Farli's life already, and it doesn't sit well in my gut. I know what it's like, first hand, when someone invades a peaceful land and brings unwanted technology with them. And it makes my blood run cold to think of Farli losing the happy innocence in her demeanor.

I'm going to do my damnedest to protect that.

CHAPTER 4

MARDOK

I HAVE TO FINISH UP my work outside, because leaving the parts scattered in the bloody snow isn't a good idea. I leave Farli with Niri and go back to my task. I clean up the engine as best I can, but I'm distracted. It's impossible to work without thinking of Farli and her wide-eyed wonder. She's beautiful, and there's something so pure about her that I feel…hungry for. I'm the last one she should get involved with, but I feel like we're connected nevertheless. And I think about her when the distant twin suns go down and the air grows even colder. Farli was naked in this. How did she not freeze her damned ass off? It's a mystery to me, though I know it has to do with the symbiont she carries that makes her eyes blue and her skin radiate warmth.

By the time I clean up the engine and take a quick shower in my quarters, it's time for the captain's dinner. I head into med bay, but it's empty of both women, the only occupant the still-sleeping furry animal. At least it's still breathing and its vitals are good. I heave a sigh of relief at that. Least she can't hate me for killing her pet.

For some reason, it's really important to me that she not hate me.

I head to the mess hall, and the formal dining table has been unfolded from the wall. I inwardly cringe, thinking of Farli sitting at dinner in nothing but her loincloth. Is the captain trying to embarrass her? Or us? Put the little savage in her place in the hopes that he can wring out the 'truth' of why Farli showed up? I don't think she's hiding anything. I don't think she could. I think she's as guileless and innocent as she seems, and I get angrier and angrier at the thought of the captain trying to force her into some sort of ridiculous confession by embarrassing her or putting her out of her element.

All of that changes the moment I see her, of course.

She's smiling. Of course she is. Farli seems to love everything, and the fascination of the dining hall setup is no different. Her eyes are wide with excitement as a nearby bot sets the table and drinks are poured. Niri's talking to her, but I suspect Farli isn't listening. She's trying to take in everything around her, from the holo on the wall that shows pastoral landscape scenes, to the silverware placed on the elegant table, to the smells filling the room. She looks more beautiful than before, too. She's wearing one of Niri's extra jumpsuits, and it doesn't quite fit her like it does Niri's lanky form. It's tight across the bust and too small through the arms and thighs, because Farli's far more muscular than the rail-thin medic. It looks almost indecent, and as if Niri has realized this, the jumpsuit is open in the front, revealing a sliver of borrowed under-tunic. Layers, so she doesn't look as if she's busting out of the top. Smart. Farli's thick, wild hair has been pulled back into a ponytail knotted high at the crown of her head, and her bare, unadorned horns look as prominent as her beaming smile.

Her attention turns the moment I approach, and I can hear her purring. Niri's eyebrows go up, and she moves away, programming drink stations at each seat. "Mardok," Farli exclaims at the sight of me. Her eyes light up. "You have returned." She moves toward me and puts her arms around my waist, tucking her head against my shoulder. She inhales deeply. "And you have bathed. What is this marvelous smell?"

"It's ah…just the ship's generic soap." I pat her back awkwardly, glancing at Niri. Her mouth is thin with disapproval, and I'm not sure if it's for me or for Farli. Probably me. She likely thinks I'm taking advantage of Farli. And certain parts of me are very, very okay with that idea. So I reluctantly pull her away. "Why don't you have a seat? I can show you how to operate the drink menu."

For the next few minutes, while we wait for the captain and Trakan, I demonstrate how the drink station operates. Niri's already got it set up, but I show her anyhow, and she orders several different things just to taste them, grabbing her glass before it finishes filling and making a mess. A bot immediately slides onto the table to clean it up, which causes even more excitement, and after that, I think Farli deliberately spills things just to see the reaction. Niri doesn't approve, but I love the childlike wonder in Farli's face and the way she wrinkles her nose when she tastes everything. She doesn't like beer, or fermented milk. She doesn't like the fizzy drinks that Trakan is addicted to, or the bitter stims that I chug on late nights. In the end, she settles on water.

The captain appears, and I jump to my feet. So does Niri. Farli watches us with fascination but does not leave her seat.

"You stand when the captain appears," Niri tells her.

Farli blinks. "Why?"

"Because that is what you do." Niri seems impatient with

Farli's endless questions.

Farli looks to me, curious. I shrug and give her a nod, and this seems to infuriate Niri even more. Not my fault that Farli wants me to guide her instead of Niri. She gets to her feet, and the captain moves toward his chair, his hands clasped behind his back. He ignores the rest of us, like he always does. Behind him is Trakan, and his eyes are devouring Farli's lithe form in the tight jumper.

That protective surge rises in my gut, and I have to fight the urge not to jump in front of her and shield her from his eyes. I glare at him, hoping he keffing notices that I don't like the way he's looking at her.

The captain sits. Niri and I sit down, too, and Farli does a moment later, though it's clear she doesn't understand the ceremony. Trakan immediately glides over to her side, extending his hand. "Well, well, Niri told me that we had a visitor, but I didn't believe her. Hard to think that a beauty like you is hiding out on this iceball of a planet."

Farli looks delighted at his words, but she ignores his hand. "You are speaking my language!"

"Niri sent us the language file so we could all chat. I look forward to hearing more of what you have to say." He winks at her and nudges his hand closer. I notice his tail is flicking in a rather predatory fashion, and anger burns in my gut. He's got a girl back at spaceport. He needs to leave Farli alone.

She eyes his hand and then looks at me. Maybe it's me being an ass, but I shake my head, indicating she should ignore it.

"Gonna be like that, huh?" I can't tell if Trakan's talking to me or to her, but it doesn't matter. I lean in so I'm closer to her and give him a challenging stare.

He smirks at me and moves to his seat, across from Farli.

"It is a pleasure to meet you," the captain says in an austere tone as he presses the button to begin the first course. "Why don't you tell us why you are here?"

She looks at me, and then her brows crease in a frown. "I was hunting."

"Here on this planet," the captain amends smoothly as the first course is served. Bowls of kelp soup are placed in front of us, and the others begin to eat, delicate eating sticks clinking against the bowls.

Farli sniffs over her soup and then looks at me again, a distressed expression on her face. I take my eating sticks in hand slowly and take a mouthful with exaggerated motions. She picks up the sticks at her side and examines them, then lifts one to her nose to sniff.

Trakan snorts with muffled laughter.

I scowl at him.

"I am not sure what you mean, here on this planet," Farli says as she tries to balance the sticks between her fingers like I am. After a moment she gives up, uses one stick to fish out a stewed leaf, and takes a small bite—and immediately I can tell she hates the food. She chews for a long time, and I try to think up what excuse I can give if she spits it out, but she swallows bravely and then sets her eating sticks down. "I live here."

"Do many of your people live here?" Chatav asks.

"Oh, all of them."

Trakan chokes another laugh off, hiding behind his drink.

"And how many is that?" the captain asks smoothly, and I hate this. I hate that he's interrogating her and she's got no clue of what he's doing, because she doesn't have a bit of guile in her body.

She gives a bright little laugh. "I cannot count that high. At least ten hands worth, and that does not include the humans."

"Humans?"

"Yes. They came here several seasons ago. The bad aliens left them here, and my chief found Shorshie and the others and rescued them. They are all mated to good strong hunters now. They all have kits, too. Some have several." Her expression goes from pleasant to slightly wistful, and I notice she's looking at me again.

"Tell me more about the humans," the captain says. "They are stranded here like your people?"

"No, they live here like us." She talks happily about the different 'mated' people in her tribe and the personalities of the 'humans.' I see Niri pull out her personal pad and begin to type, while Trakan and Chatav eat their soup. Farli does not eat, just talks, and it is clear she has great affection for everyone in her 'tribe.'

In a break in the conversation, Niri murmurs, "Humans are life forms from Sol III, Captain. Primitive culture. D-class planet."

"Kef," Trakan says, pushing his bowl aside. "D-class life forms, too? I hope we're not touching that with a ten-foot pole."

I know what he's thinking. Niri looks uneasy, too. Planets with a 'D' classification are off limits to any and all contact. If we're found with contraband aliens, we could get nailed for kidnapping, even if we aren't the responsible parties. A tricky situation just got trickier.

The captain doesn't look worried. He finishes his soup, and the bowls are cleared away. I've barely eaten mine—no appetite. Farli's is barely touched. New plates are set out, this time delicate little veg-cakes garnished with fanciful spirals. I watch as Farli's nostrils flare, and she makes no move to eat this, either.

"So your people and the humans arrived at the same time?" Chatav continues. "Together?"

"No. We have always been here. The humans came a few seasons ago." She's starting to get frustrated with the conversation, it's clear. "Why?"

"I'm just trying to figure out the best way to proceed from here." I imagine the captain's mentally running numbers on how much it'll cost us to dump our cargo and pick up at least forty refugees, some of them D-class. Trakan's no longer laughing, and Nisi looks upset. They're seeing their pay slip away, and normally I'd be upset, too. But Farli's more important to me than a few credits.

"Proceed? What do you mean?" Farli looks at me.

I nod at her plate. "You should eat."

She leans closer, and as she does, she starts to purr again. Her expression goes soft as she looks at me, and then she whispers, "Will we get meat soon?"

"Meat?" I ask, surprised.

"Meat?" The captain echoes, appalled. "You eat animal flesh?"

I can see Farli cringe back in her seat, and that protective feeling surges through me again. "Not sure what else she's supposed to eat while she's here, Captain. Didn't see a lot of farms or processing plants out in that snow."

"Mm." He still looks repulsed.

I shoot Farli a reassuring glance. "We don't have meat, I'm sorry. Maybe we can find something else for you."

Her smile in my direction is dazzling, and it almost makes up for Trakan's quiet snickering. I reach under the table and squeeze her hand. I'll make sure she gets what she needs.

***

FARLI

By the time the endless, strange meal is finished, I am ravenously hungry and exhausted all at once. I have never talked so much at one time and yet managed to say so very little. Every time I spoke, the sly-looking male would smirk. Niri would frown. And the other one—Cap-tan—would just throw more questions at me and misunderstand everything I said. I feel frustrated and tired, and I need to ask for fire, even though I haven't seen any since arriving. It is a long way back to the closest hunter cave in the dark, and I'll need a torch.

I return to the healer's room with Niri after the eating, and check on Chahm-pee. He is still asleep, but he snores like he always does, and I feel a little better seeing that. I sit at his side on one of the strange stools and stroke his furry nose. I am not sure if I am comforting him or myself. These strangers are…odd and not entirely pleasant. I do not understand why they make me feel…like less. It is a sensation I have never felt before. The sly one laughed all through his meal, and I sometimes got the impression he was laughing at me. I have always imagined what I would do if I met strangers like Vektal met the humans, and I never pictured them being…unpleasant.

All except Mardok, of course.

My mate.

I give a dreamy sigh, picturing his face. He is stern but protective. He tried to make me comfortable throughout the strange meal, and when the others made faces at my words, he scowled at them. I liked that. I think my mother would like Mardok, too. I cannot wait to return to the village and introduce him to the others. I am so proud of how handsome and strong he is. My khui has chosen wisely, and we will make adorable kits together.

As if my thoughts have summoned him, Mardok appears in the healer's room, looking around. He pauses when he sees me, a faint look of relief on his face. "There you are."

"I followed Niri," I tell him, and stroke Chahm-pee's nose again. "I wanted to see if he was well before I left."

"Left? You're leaving?" Mardok is shocked.

"Once I get fire for a torch. I will be back in the morning to check on my fat one here." I lovingly smooth my fingers down Chahm-pee's brow.

"Are you going home?"

"No." I give him a puzzled glance as I stand. "I am out hunting. My home is many days' travel away."

"Hunting alone?"

"Of course. Some hunt with their mates, but I have not had the opportunity," I say, feeling shy. Should I point out to him now that we are mated? That even now, I am resonating to him because I wish for our bodies to join together? It does not feel like the right time. Not yet, with Niri in the next chamber.

"Fire?" he echoes thoughtfully, then shakes his head. "I can give you an electronic light source, but it'd be easier if you stayed here overnight."

Here with him? He's finally inviting me to touch him? Pleased, I move forward eagerly. "I would love to share your furs."

His expression grows stiff. "No, Farli, that's not what I meant." He clasps my hands in his, but gives a small shake of his head. "I would not use you like that. You can have my room, and I'll sleep in the storage locker."

I pay no attention to most of that. Use me? Use me how? I would love to mate with him, but he is gazing down at me like it is a terrible idea, and I do not understand why. "You want me to sleep in your furs, but not with you?"

"Just to give you someplace safe to sleep."

He gazes down at me, and the expression on his face is hungry—just for a flash, but it's there. And I feel a little better. He is attracted to me, I think, but does not know how to handle it. Maybe with his people it is not appropriate to show interest? I do not know any of the rules and feel a little lost.

"All right," I say softly.

Mardok glances over at Niri, who is watching us. "Farli's going with me," he tells her. "If you need her or her pet wakes up, buzz my room."

She nods, and her mouth thins out again. "I'll let the captain know."

"You do that." His tone is short, and I am puzzled again. I thought they were friends.

Mardok leads me out of the room and down a series of dark, narrow halls. It smells like the Elders' Cave in here, that strange hard scent that Har-loh calls 'metal.' We turn down another passageway, and I hear the sound of voices, in the strange language. Mardok halts and tucks me behind him, against the wall, and listens to the others.

It must be the two males I met at dinner. The elder and the sly one. I did not care for either, and I feel ashamed about that. Perhaps they just need time to adjust to me, like the humans needed time to adjust to living on our world. I should not dislike them just because they made me feel foolish at their strange dinner. In their strange way, they were trying to be polite.

I think.

But Mardok does not seem to be in a hurry to leave. He is attentively listening to them, and since I cannot understand them, I focus on him. The muscles on his neck and shoulders are covered with a thin tunic, but I remember the sight of all that blue skin and the drawings underneath. This close, I can see the lines of his skull where it meets his thick neck, and admire the shiny covers on his horns. I put a hand on his back, because the scent of him this close is irresistible, and I feel him stiffen at my touch. I can hear his breathing speed up. It sends an answering pulse of excitement through my body, and my khui grows louder, so loud that I feel it is shaking my entire chest with its enthusiasm.

He puts a finger to his lips, indicating quiet. As if I can control my khui? It chooses who to sing to, not me. I do not say this aloud, of course. Instead, I find myself staring at his raised hand. It is the arm that is capped with the shiny stone, like his horns are, and I wonder what the story is behind that. His tail flicks against my leg, its shortened length holding a story of its own.

This male is so full of stories, of mysteries. I cannot wait to find them all out. I sigh happily and press my cheek to his shoulder, pleased. I have not felt this right about a male, ever. The moment I saw him, I knew he was mine. This is why I have never had interest in Taushen, or Sessah. I have been waiting all this time for my Mardok. I slide my arms around his waist, holding him close and breathing in his scent. It does not matter that he is cooler to the touch or that his people are strange. He is mine.

The talking dies away, and Mardok's hand covers mine, pressing against his stomach. "We can go now. My quarters are just down the hall."

Does this mean I have to let him go? I pull away from him, and the only thing that makes me happy about that is that he seems reluctant to let me go also.

He takes me by the hand and leads me onward. "What were they talking about?" I ask him, keeping my voice hushed.

Mardok stops at a panel full of lights and begins to tap at buttons. "They were discussing options."

"Options?"

My mate glances over his shoulder at me. "We're not equipped to be a rescue ship. They're trying to figure out if we've got enough food or fuel to bring your people with us, and if we do, what happens to our cargo we've already been paid for."

I do not follow some of his words, and shake my head. "Go with you? Go with you where?"

The wall opens, pulling back to reveal a small chamber. In it, I see several large, square objects I do not recognize, and one I do—his furs. This must be where he sleeps. The walls are bare of any pleasant hangings, and the floor has no furs to block the cold. It looks very bare and unfriendly, this cave, and I feel sad for him that he must spend his time in such a place.

He pulls me inside, and the wall shuts behind him. I look around, hugging my arms. It is overwarm in here, like it is in every chamber of this ship. "Do you live here by yourself?"

"Yeah. The others have their own private chambers. We're a small ship, but not that small." He moves past me and begins to straighten things on a flat surface—more strange, square shapes. His people must love squares. "I'm sorry the place is a mess."

"Is it?"

Mardok flashes me a grin and then hurriedly straightens the thin-looking bed furs, then indicates I should sit there. I do, and he sits down across from me on the only stool in the chamber, spinning around. "I'm sorry dinner was such a shitshow."

I do not know the word, but the meaning is clear. "I did not know your customs. I apologize—"

Mardok looks angry at my words. He leans forward and clasps my hand in his. "There is nothing to apologize for, Farli. The captain did not believe your story, and I think it was all a test. And Trakan? He's just an asshole. Don't let them get to you."

My khui begins to sing a soft song as I become acutely aware of my hand in his. "I will not. But...where do they want to take my people?"

Now Mardok looks confused. "Away from here. Your people are stranded."

Are we? I had no idea. "I see. I would need to talk it over with my chief." I am not entirely sure I like the idea, though he and his people seem to think it is a done deal. "Where would we go?"

"Well, I imagine you'd need to go to Homeworld first. That's a planet called Kes. It's where our people come from, and it's the seat of everything. You'd have to go there. Get your records established. From there, I guess you could go to my planet. It's nice. Lots of green trees, clear waters, many beaches."

I think of the food at dinner—bland and tasteless. I glance around this chamber, all squares and empty walls. I think of how the others acted at dinner. And I do not want to hurt his feelings, so I just smile. It is clear to me that he will need to live with us, instead of me going to live with him. "Your family is on your world?"

His expression grows distant. He lets go of my hand and sits back. "I don't have any family left."

My heart aches for him. "Did you lose them to a sickness? Over twenty turns of the seasons ago, we lost a great many in our tribe to the khui-sickness. I am lucky in that I did not lose my parents or my brothers, but I know many who did."

"Did you get sick?" he asks me, clearly trying to steer the conversation back toward me.

"I did not. I was a young kit. Very young. My khui was new

and strong, I think. Perhaps that helped."

"Your symbiont?" He leans forward, scooting his stool closer to me, and his gaze fixes on my eyes. I feel the heat pulse through my body again, and I wish he would take my hand once more. I want to put it on my teat again and see if he responds how he did before or if he is interested. Even if he does not resonate to me—yet—I am content to pleasure-mate with him. He is the first male I have wanted to even try it with. Ever since I met him, I can think of nothing but what it would feel like to have him touch me. "Can you feel it inside you?" he asks.

I nod. "Only at certain times. Like now, when it is singing." I put my hand over my chest. I do not tell him why it is singing. Not yet.

He gives me a slow smile, so stunningly handsome that it takes my breath away. "Singing, eh? I like that." But then his smile fades. "Farli...I just want to apologize to you for what happened earlier."

"At dinner?"

"No, not dinner, though someone should definitely apologize for that." He grimaces and rubs his brow. "For what happened with you...and your pet."

I tilt my head, curious. "What happened with me and my pet? Something hurt him. It happens. This world is not safe." I did not see what it was, other than a flash of light.

The look on his face is full of distress, and it makes my heart hurt. "It was me."

A knot forms in my throat. "You...what?"

"I saw him charging out of the corner of my eye, and I just... reacted." His eyes are mere slits, his expression haunted. "I...I flashed back to when I was a soldier. Fired without thinking. I'm sorry."

I do not know what to say. I am aching inside. He was the

one that hurt my poor Chahm-pee. The thought fills me with wounded rage…and yet it is clear from his expression that it was an accident. "I see."

Mardok gets up. "Listen, I've probably been in your ear too much already. I'll leave you alone to get some sleep. You're probably tired."

Tired? Not in the slightest. Not with my body humming at his presence and my heart full of conflicting emotions. But all I know is that he did not mean it, and he has done everything he can to make Chahm-pee better. "It is all right, Mardok."

"It's not. I'm all keffed in the head." He heaves a sigh and moves to the wall. "Better that I leave you alone. You'll be comfortable in here by yourself."

"You are leaving?" I do not want him to go. Not now. Not ever.

"I need to." The look on his face is full of self-loathing, and surprising to me. "Been here a day and I'm keffing up your life. I need to take a step back. Leave you alone."

Leave me alone? "I do not want to be alone, Mardok."

"You'll be fine. Get some sleep." He moves to the wall and gestures at a panel. "I'll be asleep in the storage room next door. Just hit this red button if you get scared and I'll come find you."

Scared? Of the dark? Like a kit? I bite back my amusement, because he's leaving and I want him to stay. "Do not go, Mardok."

But he only shakes his head and taps the panel. The wall opens, and he leaves. After a moment, the wall closes again, and I am in his chamber, alone. The novelty of it lasts only a brief moment. I explore his room, touching his things, trying to learn more about him from them. I see no signs of family, no extra tunics or carefully kept toys from siblings grown up. The squares on his desk are puzzling—they open up to nothing but a bunch of white slips with black squiggles on them. I pick one up, smell it, and then put it down again. Smells musty. His furs smell like him, and I climb onto the raised platform of his bedding to wallow in them. Then, when I am tired of sniffing his scent, I get up and approach the panel.

I hit the red button. Something beeps. "I'm coming," Mardok's voice calls through the wall, and it sounds strange and hollow. I press my ear to the door, curious. "Where are you? I hear you but do not see you."

The wall next to me pulls back, and Mardok steps through, looking worried. "Are you all right?"

I pat the wall I have my hands on. "I heard your voice here. How did you get over there?"

His mouth twitches. "I'm not in the wall. That was the intercom."

"Can we do it again?" I am fascinated. "I want to hear your voice."

He shakes his head. "Go to sleep. If you're not scared or you don't need anything, sleep. We'll talk in the morning."

Humph. I say nothing as he leaves. The moment the wall shuts, I hit the button again.

There's a long pause. "Mardok?" I yell into the wall, where his voice came from earlier. "I wish to speak to you." I hit the button again, then call out, "Come and talk to me."

This time, the wall does not speak with his voice. The panel opens and he steps inside again, crossing his arms over his chest like I am a naughty kit. "Farli?"

I beam a smile at him. "You are back."

"Because you won't stop pushing the button." He leans against the entrance and sighs heavily. "Are you scared?"

I clasp my hands in front of my chest. "If I say I am, will you stay and talk to me?"

Mardok glances down the hall one way, then the other. Satisfied, he steps inside and lets the panel slide shut behind him. "I shouldn't be here."

"Yes, you should." My khui begins to sing immediately. This is the perfect place for him to be—with me.

"The captain's going to have my ass if he finds out." But he moves past me and heads to one of the squares on the wall, and pulls out extra furs and a pillow. Oh. The squares are storage baskets. How odd. He takes the strange, flat furs and spreads them on the ground next to the bed. "I'll sleep here, okay? So you won't be scared."

I should tell him that I am not scared now, but he will leave. So I just smile brightly at him and move to my bed. "You can sleep up here with me."

"No," he says, amusement in his voice. "No, I really can't. Trust me."

"I will not take up much room. I promise."

"No."

"I am a light sleeper. I will not snore or lash you with my tail—"

"Farli, no. Okay? Just no." He lies down and fluffs a pillow behind his head. "Go to sleep. Lie down."

He is determined to send me to bed like a kit, is he not? Frustrating. I lie back in the bed and stare up at the ceiling.

"Lights off," Mardok says in a low voice.

The entire room dims and grows dark.

I gasp, sitting up. "How—" I am filled with wonder. "Lights on," I call out, hoping it'll respond.

"This room is programmed to my voice. Sorry. Get under the covers and go to sleep." Mardok says. "I can show you how everything works in the morning."

I lie back again, but it is stifling hot and I am wearing far too many layers for sleeping. Get under the furs? I will sweat *a lake if I do.* I stare up, wishing Mardok was here with me and wishing he was not so determined to ignore me. Still, if I am to be ignored, at least I can be cooler. I undo the ties at my waist and begin to peel off Niri's borrowed tunic with the legs built in. If he notices my squirming atop the blankets and their strange platform, he does not say anything. I think he is trying to ignore me to sleep. I finish stripping off the leathers and feel a little cooler. I am still wearing a fine sheen of sweat, but at least my skin can breathe. I blink in the darkness, thinking about my dvisti. "Do you think Chahm-pee is all right?"

"He's fine. Niri's got him all patched up. The only thing med bay can't reproduce quickly is artificial blood, but that should be taken care of by morning." I hear his blankets rustle as he turns over. "Do you…need to be somewhere? Will your parents be looking for you?"

I chuckle. "Not likely. I have been hunting on my own since I had my first flow."

He's quiet. Then, "Uh, if you don't mind me asking, how old are you exactly?"

I am amused by the question…but only for a brief moment. Then I realize what it means. He thinks I am a kit. Is this why he pushes me away constantly? He worries I should be at the teat and not trying to claim him as my mate? I swallow my hurt. "I have seen the seasons turn over twenty-two times."

"And the years are longer here, right?" He exhales deeply. "Thank gods. I was worried for a moment there."

"How old are you?" I taunt him back.

"Thirty-eight years by my world's reckoning. I guess I'd be a little over thirty-five of yours."

I snort. "Barely old enough to be a hunter yourself." In truth, he is young but in his prime—the perfect age for me. Maybe I'm a little wounded that he thinks I am a silly kit, after all. Is this how Sessah feels around me? I must remember to be nicer to him.

"A hunter, huh?" He chuckles into the dark, and the sound is warm and delicious. "I like that. Beats being a soldier."

His laughter feels like a caress, and I hate that I am up here on this platform and he is down there. Why can we not be in the furs together? I will gladly sweat in this heat if it means I can touch him. He is just below me, and if I were on the ground, we would be close enough to touch.

On impulse, I move to the edge of the bed and then roll off the side. I land on his chest, and my forehead knocks into his. My khui's song increases.

"Ooof," he groans, and then touches my arm. "Are you okay, Farli? Did you fall off?"

"I wanted to visit," I say. I am breathless with excitement at how close we are. I can taste his scent on the air, and it is making me aroused. My khui just sings and sings, pleased I have found my mate.

Mardok pats my arm, and then he hesitates. His hand moves up to my shoulder, and then his breath hisses out of his lungs. "Are you...naked?"

"It is hot in here," I tell him. "Too hot to sleep. Is naked a problem? My people are naked whenever they please." I put my hands on his shoulders. Still clothed. Hmm. If we are going to mate, he is going to need to take some layers off.

"Naked is only a problem if it's been three years," he mutters.

"It is just skin."

"Farli, I shouldn't be here." He very gently tries to pry me off of him. "I'm flattered—hell, I'm attracted to you like crazy, too, but we can't do this."

I ignore his words, focusing on what I like. "You are attracted to me, too?" It makes me wiggle with pleasure.

He groans, and his hands go to my shoulders, as if trying to hold me still. "Stop moving like that. You're going to kill me."

I brush his hands off and lean in, letting my fingers trace his features in the dark. He's not pushing me away, so I grow bolder. "You like me?" I repeat again. I need to hear him say the words. "You do not think I am too young?"

"I think you're just too keffing innocent, that's all. I don't want to be the one that spoils that."

"You spoil nothing," I tell him, and let my fingers wander over his lips. They are surprisingly soft for all of the frowns he tends to do over a day. "Let me be in control of my innocence."

I can feel him smile under my fingertips. I want to put my mouth there again, to do the mouth-matings and see how he reacts now that we know each other. Will he touch me back this time? I hope so. I slide forward, moving up his chest just a little, and lean forward until my nose bumps against his.

"Farli," he murmurs. I do not know if it is a protest or encouragement. I will take it as encouragement.

My khui is singing wildly as I bend my head and brush my lips over his. He is motionless underneath me, and so I increase the kiss, letting my lips move over his. I have seen how the others mouth-mate and know that tongues are involved, so I let mine play along the seam of his mouth. He parts his lips, and I take the opportunity to flick my tongue against his.

It feels as if a fire has sparked in my body. Need surges through me, and every nerve ending responds to the feel of his body under mine, his mouth against mine. He hesitates, only for a moment, and then his hands are in my mane and he's holding me against him as our mouths slant together, our tongues locked in a dance. His tail flicks under the blankets, and a moment later, I feel it wrap around mine. My body is humming with need, and my teats feel tight and achy, and there is a hot pulse between my thighs that will not go away. Over and over, his tongue flicks against mine, until we are both breathless and panting.

"Well," he says between breaths. "I'm pretty sure we just broke a hygiene law on at least three different planets."

I giggle. I have no idea what he just said, but I like the wonder in his voice. "It was a good mouth-mating, yes? I liked it. We should do it more."

He groans. "Have mercy. I won't be able to control myself if you do that again. Give me a moment to compose myself." His hands stroke my mane again and then slide down my sides. "Gods, you are really, really naked."

I wiggle on top of him, because I am pleased with how this is going. I loved kissing him. It was so fun, and it has made me so aroused. I want to do it more. "I really, really am." I lean down and lick the tip of his nose, just because I want to lick him everywhere.

"Where did you learn to do that with your mouth?"

"Humans taught me. It is common on their planet. Is it not on yours?"

"No. Kef, I think I've only seen stuff like that in vids. Most mesakkah women aren't quite so…open. They're worried about disease. Mouths are so unclean."

"Pfft. Do you think my mouth is unclean?" I press another kiss to his lips.

"I think your mouth is amazing," he murmurs. His hand slides along my flank and then lightly caresses my buttock. "I've never met anyone like you, Farli."

I preen under the compliment and give another wiggle. He sucks in a breath, and I realize the hard ridge I am straddling is not his hip but his cock. Oh. My body flushes with heat, and I rock my hips over him experimentally. It drags his blanket-covered length against my folds, and the sensation is dizzying.

Mardok groans again, and then, sky-claw fast, he wraps his arms around me and rolls until I am at his side and not straddling him. We face each other, so close the curves of our horns are practically touching and I can feel his breath on my face. "Tell me you're real," he says to me. "I feel like if I go to sleep, I'm going to wake up and this will all have been a dream."

"I am very real," I tell him, and trace my fingers over his cheek again. "Why do you have drawings on your face?"

"They're tattoos. I got them when I was…" He hesitates. "When I was in the military. At war."

"What is military?"

"Nothing good." His tone has changed. It's no longer sensual and full of pleasure, but turning cold. This is something that hurts him. I decide to change the topic, letting my fingers glide up his arching horns and along the curve. "Why are your horns shiny?"

He gives a short, breathless laugh. "You're very curious, aren't you?"

"Mm. It is because you are a very curious man." But the darkness is creeping out of his voice, so I am happy. I want nothing but his smiles. Whatever bad things are in his past, I will make better for him with my love. "Is it a secret?"

"No, it's custom. People cap their horns because…well, I don't know. It's just what you do. I guess it's polite. Keeps you from accidentally scratching someone if you move wrong." I can feel him shrug. "I've never met anyone without capped horns except you."

"I am special," I tease. "You like that."

"You're very special." The husky note is back in his voice, and I wish his eyes glowed in the dark like mine so I could see them. He is just...dark. *Soon enough he will have a khui,* I remind myself.

"Can we kiss more?" I ask him, snuggling closer. My nose rubs against his. "I like kissing you."

"We shouldn't. It's against Captain's rules to have relations with ship guests, and I'm pretty sure you qualify." But his hand glides up and down my arm, touching my bare skin, and his tail is still twined with mine. "I'll lose my position."

"What position?"

"My job."

"What is job?"

He chuckles. "Like your people have hunters. I am a mechanic. Well, that and security. I do both."

It makes no sense for him to lose his position in his small tribe because he touches me, but perhaps their customs are harsh...or he has a mate. I suck in a breath. What if he has a mate and that is why he has not resonated to me? I grab his horns with both of my hands and hold his face against mine, my brow pressing to his as if this will give me the answers faster. "Mardok," I say quickly. "Do you have a mate?"

"A what?"

"A female? A mate? A family? Kits?"

"What? No. I told you, I'm a soldier. *Was* a soldier." I can feel his heavy sigh in the air between us. "It keffed my head up good. Can't bring a family into that. Never wanted to."

I am relieved. "Good."

"Why good?" He sounds amused.

"Because you are my mate and no one else's."

There's a long pause. "What?"

I put my hand to his chest. Still covered in his silly, thin leathers. He should be naked with me. "You are my mate and I am yours. We have resonated."

CHAPTER 5

MARDOK

MATE?

I wonder if this is one of the language gaps and I'm not hearing her right. Or maybe it's hard to concentrate when her gorgeous, supple body is pressing up against mine and she's completely naked, her skin scorchingly hot and slightly damp. It makes me picture what she looks like in the light, all blue curves, skin gleaming, her thick hair wild over her shoulders, those bare horns…I have to suppress a shudder or I'm going to take myself in hand, right here. I need to focus on what she's saying. "You say resonance. What does that mean?"

Her nose brushes against mine, and I think she's going to put her lips on me again. I've never experienced anything like her mouth-on-mouth kiss before. I've seen it in the kind of vids that no decent woman ever watches. And I've read about it, but I've never actually done it. All of the women I've had relationships with in the past have been brought up by modern society, concerned more with hygiene and disease control than the intimacy of putting her mouth on me. I've rarely even touched bare skin. But Farli? She is unafraid and unashamed of who she is, and she revels in caresses and the touches that everyone else I know would eschew.

It makes touching her have a forbidden feel to it, even moreso given the captain's longstanding ship orders. I know if we're caught together, I'll be dumped at the nearest port and given severance. That doesn't mean I can stop stroking her soft skin or that I can push her away when she rubs up against me like a nilu cat seeking attention.

"Resonance?" she murmurs, her voice sweet and soft. Her hand glides over my arm and down my chest, and she presses her palm against the cartilage plates there. "It begins here. The khui sings a song to let me know when I have met my mate."

"Singing?" I press my hand between her breasts, to the same place she's touching me. "Here? When you purr?" Even now, I can feel the vibrations in her chest. It doesn't sound like a song to me, more of a low-pitched, steady thrumming. It does sound a little musical, now that I think about it. "So what do you mean by mated?"

She chuckles, and I feel her tongue flick along my jaw, tracing the lines of it. Gods above, but she's sensual. "What do you think it means?"

"Sex," I say bluntly, and the stub of my tail tightens its obsessive grip around hers. "Lots and lots of sex. But I'm guessing there is more than that."

"I will tell you if we can kiss again," she teases, and nuzzles my nose again. Her hand moves up my shirt, fingers sneaking into my collar so she can touch my skin. I don't think she can figure out the fastenings, because she tugs at the front of my clothing and then gives up. I should push her away, but everything in me wants more of her innocent touches, more exploring and caressing. I pull my shirt open, and she responds with a happy sigh, her hands moving over my chest, exploring me.

"You want kisses?" I ask, brushing my hand over her hair. I move my body slightly, until she's under me and I'm over her, leaning on an elbow. The primal male in me wants her under me. Doesn't matter how wrong it is. I want to claim her innocence, even if only for a moment. I take the lead on the kiss this time, tasting her luscious mouth, and when she opens for me, I drag my tongue against hers. She makes a soft mewling noise of pleasure, and I feel it all the way down to my cock.

Mine. She's mine.

I can fight it all I want, but I know that she belongs to me. My kiss grows more possessive, my mouth more aggressive as she responds under me. She arches, pressing her breasts to my chest, and her hard little nipples scrape against my shirt. I nearly come at that smallest of touches. I keep my hands respectfully on her arm and in her hair, though I want nothing more than to slide my fingers over her pussy and see if it's soaking wet for me. I bet it is.

I abandon her mouth with one final, suggestive lick, and she pants, dazed. "You are very good at that, Mardok."

"I had a good teacher."

"Who?"

I nip at her lower lip, drawing another shudder from her. "You."

"Oh," she says, shy. "Am I your first, too?"

My first? "First what?"

"First mating?"

Does she mean having sex? "I've had sex before. Uh, fornicated." Damn, even the word sounds too filthy to use when it comes to her. Farli would never fornicate. She would make love. Hell, and now I sound like a lovesick poet. "Not in a long time, though. Haven't wanted anyone to touch me."

I feel her fingertips dance over my chest. "Is it all right if I touch you?"

I think I'd die if she stopped. I swallow hard. "Yeah."

"You will be my first," she tells me. "I have waited for my mate."

Just like that, my heart stutters. "Your first…mate?" Is she a virgin? When she nods, I groan and press my forehead to hers. She's more innocent than I thought, and I wonder if she's going to regret being here with me, touching me. Doing lascivious things with her mouth. I'm craving her like Trakan craves his carcinogels, but I'm not an asshole. Very slowly, I detangle my tail from hers and pull her hands away from my chest. I press my mouth to one palm. "Maybe you should go back home and wait to resonate to another nice guy, the one you want to marry."

She's quiet, and then she gives another light giggle. "You only resonate to one person ever, silly."

What? "Are we talking about the same thing? I'm talking about sex."

"I am talking about resonating. When your khui chooses someone for you."

Farli's throwing me mixed signals here. "If it chooses for you, I don't understand what you mean by 'you waited.'"

"Mating with someone is nothing," Her tail flicks on the blankets, and I wonder if she's growing frustrated with me. "People take pleasure-mates all the time. It is like…scratching an itch. But you only resonate to your true mate." Her fingers touch my chin again, as if she is trying to force me to concentrate. "Like I said, the khui chooses. It selects the male and the female that will be best together so it can bring about the strongest kits."

Whoa, whoa, whoa. Everything inside me screeches to a halt. I swallow hard. "Kits?"

"Yes. The khui chooses the perfect person to father my young. It always chooses, and it chooses well." I can practically hear her smiling in the dark. All the while, her chest is doing that thrumming, purring thing. "I have waited for resonance, because I have waited for my mate. I have had offers to share my furs, but it has never interested me…until now."

Because she wants to make babies? Somehow, I don't think that's it. She really believes that if she purrs to me that we're somehow destined to be together and I'm going to make her pregnant? That's the craziest thing. I don't know what to make of it.

I also don't know what to make of the jealous surge that rises in me at the thought of her getting all kinds of offers to 'share her furs.' I shouldn't be this possessive of her, this fast. Maybe she's right about the 'resonance' thing, but I'm not sure I'm grasping all of it. "But I'm not resonating, Farli."

"Not yet." She pats my chest as if to soothe me. "You do not have a khui yet."

Her parasite? "I don't think I want one."

"But…you have to." A note of panic enters her voice. "You cannot live if you do not have a khui. Those without one will sicken and die. You cannot stay here with me without one."

I remain silent. Stay…here?

On this iceball of a planet? The familiar terror lodges in my chest.

Left behind.

It won't happen. Ever. I pat Farli's shoulder awkwardly in the dark, not wanting to tell her my thoughts. I don't want to hurt her feelings. "You should get some sleep."

She doesn't fall for it. Her arms go around my neck and

she presses quick, frantic kisses to my face, as if terrified. "Mardok," she breathes. "Tell me you will stay here with me. Please. I just found you. I cannot bear to have you leave me."

I stroke her back, and lust rises inside me again. *She's naked and pressing herself against me,* I tell myself. Any man would feel hunger in this situation. But it feels different with Farli. In the past, when I was freshly discharged from the military, I'd get approached by women in spaceport bars looking for a quick, rough hookup. Some of them were far more forward than Farli is, and yet I felt…nothing for them.

I'm afraid I'm feeling too much for Farli.

At the same time, I can't imagine living in this frigid, desolate place. Being stranded here, forever. I close my eyes, pushing past the memories that threaten to rise. "I haven't seen much of your planet," I hedge. "You could come with me."

"No, I cannot. You cannot remove a khui once it has become part of you. The humans say that there is no leaving once you are here."

That sounds like even more of a death sentence. "We'll talk about it in the morning."

I expect her to protest again, but she only presses another kiss to my mouth. "Yes, in the morning I will show you my world. You will love it."

Somehow I doubt that. But I hold her close and stroke her as she settles in to sleep. I tell myself that a planet with someone like Farli on it can't be that bad…but then I keep thinking of the bitter blast of the wind striking my face the moment I opened the door. The desolate, white landscape that seemed to be nothing but shrubs and rocks and snow.

A planet I can never leave again. And I've been restless ever since I left the military. Traveling to new worlds and systems sometimes quiets my head. Sometimes. With a job as a mechanic on a long-haul space-freighter, I've seen a lot of places. Nothing has felt even close to home…not even the ship I'm on now. Sometimes I don't feel as if I have a place anywhere.

One thing's for sure, though—if I had to pick a new home-world, this sure as shit wouldn't be it.

Farli snuggles closer to me, tucking her head against my neck and sighing happily. And I feel like an ass for my dark thoughts.

"You need to get this thing out of my med bay," Niri says, her voice pleasant despite her words. "It shit all over the floor twice this morning." She's speaking our native language so Farli can't understand her, pretending to be busy on her med pad. "Not sure why you tried to save it anyhow. Do you know how much I spent on clinic supplies for this thing overnight?"

"Don't care. Take it out of my check. And speak Farli's language so she can understand us." I keep my arms crossed over my chest, trying to look as menacing as possible to shut her up. It's not that I dislike Niri—she's the closest thing I have to a friend on *The Tranquil Lady*. But I remember dinner yesterday vividly, and while she didn't exactly mock Farli…she didn't defend her, either.

Farli. I look over at her. She's wearing Niri's jumper again today, her own furry boots covering her feet. Her hair is loose around her shoulders, and her face is wreathed in smiles as her ugly, smelly pet licks her face happily. She's the most beautiful thing I've ever seen, and as I watch her hungrily, she glances over at me. Most women would blush or play coy. Farli simply gives me an equally heated look that tells me she's still thinking about last night.

And I'm the one that blushes, my ears growing hot.

"You're grumpy this morning," Niri comments. It's in

Farli's language, so at least I don't have to growl at her over that. "Not sleep well?"

"Slept fine."

"Then it must be something else." She gives me a meaningful look and then turns her head, exaggeratingly peering over at Farli. "Something like that?"

"Leave it alone, Niri." The old woman doesn't have family to fuss over, so I'm her project. Usually I don't mind, but today it irks me. Maybe because I'm still thinking about last night and the conversation about khuis and mating and being stuck here on this planet forever. I can't imagine. Every time my brain starts to go in that direction, I think of the ship taking off and leaving me behind on the surface…and my brain goes to another time, on a jungle planet, when I was left behind with my unit in hostile territory… I shudder, then fling myself off the wall, trying to shake off the memories.

Farli turns back to her pet and leans in, hugging his neck. "Are you hungry, Chahm-pee?" She pulls a root out of her bag and waves it under his nose. "I saved this for you."

The thing takes a shit even as its little tail flips back and forth happily, and Niri makes a strangled noise.

"Can't do anything about it," I tell Niri, biting back the laugh that rises in my throat. "Captain wants Farli to stick around until he has time to chat with her. That means her pet stays, too." I woke up to a message on my com from the captain, and I'd expected it to be an ass-reaming about fraternization. It wasn't, though—just a command not to let our 'guest' go until he'd had a chance to quiz her further.

I should be annoyed that he thinks I'm her keeper—I'm not one for being social, after all. But it seems right that I be the one to stay at Farli's side. I sure don't want Trakan hovering around her, and it's clear that Niri's short allotment of patience has already been exhausted. And…Farli's *mine*. The thought of anyone else even touching a hair on her head fills me with wordless rage.

I didn't resonate to you.

Not yet.

I watch Farli and her pet for a moment, thinking. "The creature's healthy?" I ask Niri.

"As if he'd never been wounded," she says grumpily. "Minus some singed hair on his flank and a stink that's going to take forever to get out of med bay."

"What about his...symbiont? His parasite?" I tap my chest, indicating my heart. "You left it in?"

Niri's thick brows draw together. "At her request, yes. Why?"

"What can you tell me about it?"

She shrugs. "I didn't really pay too much attention to it. You know, I was busy with, oh, saving my four-legged patient."

"Can you do some analyzing on it this morning? Now?"

She tucks away her stylus on her med pad and then moves toward me. "What are you getting at?" She keeps her voice low.

I want to know about resonance. I want to know if a khui can be removed. But Niri's not stupid. She'll want to know why I'm asking these things. So I shrug. "Just curious about how the biology works, that's all."

"Mmhmm. Since you're such a big biology fan," she says, sarcasm lacing her voice. "But tell you what. How about I do a medical check-up on her just to make sure everything's in working order?"

"That'd be great."

When I don't offer more than that, she shrugs and heads toward Farli. "Hey there. Mind if I run a few tests on you just to compare how your symbiont has affected your body processes compared to ours? It's for my records."

Farli looks at me, uncertainty on her face. I give her a nod, and she smiles at Niri. "All right."

I settle back against the wall, watching the two women as Niri directs Farli to sit on the med table. After a moment, Niri turns and glances over at me. "You can go at any time."

"Oh no, I would like for him to stay," Farli says.

"I'm going to need you to take your top off for at least one scan," Niri tells her. When Farli continues to look unbothered, Niri shoots me another look.

I get up and head for the door. "I need to work on the engine anyhow. Didn't finish up yesterday, and something tells me the captain will be wanting to head out soon."

"You are leaving?" There's a note of panic in Farli's voice.

"I'll just be outside, I promise. You're safe in here with Niri. If you need me, I'm very close by." She bites her lip, and another fierce surge of protectiveness rises in me. "I'm not going anywhere, Farli."

"All right." Her mouth curves into a small smile, and she starts to purr again. Now that I know what that purring means, it makes me react a hell of a lot differently than before. My cock grows hard, remembering her open-mouthed kisses and her naked body rubbing up against me last night. "I'd better suit up," I say gruffly, and head out of med bay before anyone can notice how affected I am by Farli's presence.

Working on the engine allows my mind to focus on something other than Farli. It's still keffing cold outside, but since I'm expecting it, it doesn't feel as blisteringly awful as before. I know to suit up in advance, and as I work, I check to make sure no other 'natives' show up to say hello. The leak's an easy fix once I find the leaky hose, and then it's just a matter of patching it, replacing corroded parts, and then piecing everything back together again. I head back onto the bridge, start the drives, and run diagnostics. Everything's good. Actually, everything's running even better than before, which is nice. Shows I'm not a total keffing disaster at this job. The captain must have noticed the shiver of the engines. My incoming call light flicks, and I tap the button to answer it. "Mardok here."

"How are we looking, Vendasi?"

"Problem's fixed, Captain." I study the diagnostic scrolling across my screen. "Parts have been replaced and everything's running smooth. Looks like we're good to resume our journey at any time."

"Excellent." I think that's the end of it, but then a moment later, he adds, "Come to my chambers, would you please, Vendasi? Thank you."

My mood goes from bad to worse. I have a feeling that whatever the captain's going to say, I'm not going to want to hear. "Be right there." I head through the winding passages of the ship, my thoughts dark as I try to imagine what the captain's going to say. He's going to insist Farli fly back with us, despite the fact that Farli seems to have no inclination to leave her wintry planet. He's going to suggest all of her people fly back. He's going to decide that's a bad idea and we take off without even attempting to rescue Farli and her people. None of these thoughts sit well in my gut. Farli seems happy, but what if the others want to leave? What if the captain won't take them with us? I don't like how wary both he and Trakan have been about finding Farli here. I can't help but feel like they're up to something and I'm out of the loop. If I had to choose between Farli and my crew…I'd choose Farli. The answer is instant, but I know it's the right one. I've been with the crew of *The Tranquil Lady* for four years now, but we're not close. We're all here because we're loners.

And in the space of a day, Farli has crashed through all my walls and made me think about a life outside of this cold, unfeeling ship. Made me wonder what it'd be like to have someone like her to come home to.

I knock on the captain's door, burying these thoughts. Chatav isn't a warm man, but he's fair. I need to listen to him with an open mind.

The door slides back, and I step inside. Chatav's apartments are far larger than mine, and covered with memorabilia of his time in the military back on Homeworld. Medals and plaques detailing his honorable actions are lined up like soldiers, and a flag of the regiment he was in is tacked to the wall. His furniture is heavy wood from a forested planet, carved and fitted into his chamber. Mine is the cheap disposable shit that came with the contract. Then again, this is the captain's home, and it's just a job to me. I stop in front of the captain's 'business' desk, where he likes to have private conversations with the crew in his chambers. "You wanted to talk?"

"I do. Have a seat."

I sit in the uncomfortable wood chair across from him and wait.

He is quiet for a long moment, thinking. His hands are linked across his chest, and he gazes at one of the pictures on his 'wall of valor' as if he'd rather be back there than sitting here with me. Eventually, he glances over at me. "Tea?"

I shake my head. I was in the same military service he was. I've dealt with officers in the past, and I know a diversionary tactic when I see one.

Chatav focuses his attention on me fully, all pretense of politeness gone. "How is our wild friend this morning?"

"The animal will make a full recovery, Captain."

"I meant the girl." His smile is frosty but polite.

Oh, I knew he did. I don't think she's wild, though. Untamed, yes. Fierce and exuberant, yes. Wild implies that she needs to be broken, and there's nothing about her that needs to be fixed. "Farli is well. She finds the ship strange and has mentioned leaving to go find her people."

His eyes narrow, just a hint. "She has not talked about remaining with us? Evinced any curiosity about our ship and its cargo?"

I inwardly sigh, because it's clear he still thinks she's some sort of icy spy. You can take a man out of the military, but you can't take the military out of the man. "Not at all. She has no ulterior motivation. I think she was just surprised to see us land and came by to say hello."

"Mmhmm." His jaw clenches, but he nods slowly. "I do not sense malice in her, and I would certainly hope she is as innocent as she seems." He studies me, and then continues. "I have made a decision regarding her."

I wait. Here it comes.

"We have been put in an untenable situation, I am afraid." His voice is calm, reasoned, his expression carefully neutral. "If we wait here for very long, we will lose our delivery window. However, being as that there are clearly people here, it is our duty to determine their situation. Are they stranded here against their will? Have they always been here as she claims? Are they the results of a failed colony? Or is there something else at play?"

"Could be a failed colony," I say gruffly. You hear about that sort of thing sometimes.

"That was my first thought, as well. So I pulled any and all charter records for this planet." He shakes his head. "There's nothing. It's been classified as C-class—inhabitable, in theory. The weather's atrocious, the atmosphere's got traces of poison, and there's too much seismic activity to risk a dome colony. Not that it couldn't work, of course, but feasibly, it'd be far too expensive and remote for most charters. Just the fuel costs to bring supplies in this direction would be astronomical. And you know how much the Batenes are paying us for the kelp delivery."

I do. A keffing fortune. They're even farther out than this planet, but it's sunny and warm there. "So not a colony."

"It seems not. Which means we must ask the question why. Why are they here? Do they want to be here? Can we be of assistance in some way without compromising our shipment?" His jaw clenches again, and then he continues. "I have decided that we will need to visit her people and determine the situation after speaking with their leader."

"Determine the situation?"

"If it is a rescue situation or not. We need to know as much as possible before we decide if we are dumping our cargo to take them to the nearest station. And since our schedule is running tight already thanks to our engine troubles, we need to pay a visit to her tribe as soon as possible. We have a window of a few days at most before we need to move on if we intend on carrying out our delivery as planned."

A few days. My gut clenches at the thought. It seems like so little time. "I'm okay with losing a paycheck, just so you know. If they want to be rescued—and from talking to Farli, I'm not sure they do—then I'm on board with it. But only if they want to be rescued. I'm not forcing her—or anyone else—to go someplace they don't want to be."

"If they don't want to be rescued, that solves all my problems," Chatav says. He glances over at the picture on the wall again and then sighs heavily. "If we lose this shipment, I'm done."

I frown to myself. Done? This ship's the only thing the captain has in his life since he retired. "Pardon?"

"I'm broke," Chatav says bluntly. "Shipments have been lean, and fuel costs have gone up. I'm barely breaking even. Why do you think we're running kelp to the outer reaches of the galaxy?"

"Because it's a job?" I don't ask questions. I just go with the flow.

"Because it pays well. But every credit we spend on unnecessary fuel or repairs means our profit margin grows slimmer and slimmer. And lately there's been nothing left." He spreads his hands, and for the first time, I see a flicker of despair on his proud face. "We've been bleeding credits for a long time."

"I didn't know."

"I made sure you didn't. Hard to get crew when you're afraid you might not get paid for the next haul." He runs his hand along the wood grain of his desk. "If we don't make this shipment, I won't have the money to purchase fuel for future trips. That means if we rescue these people, we're doing the right thing and destroying ourselves in the process." His gaze meets mine. "And you're out of a job. Niri and Trakan, too. And I'll have to sell the *Lady*."

I sit back, stunned. We're not a close crew, but this is as near to stability as I've had since leaving the military. To think that it might be gone in a flash… "So what am I supposed to do?"

He shrugs. "Same thing I would, I imagine. File for government assistance."

The kef he says. Now I'm getting angry. "What about your pension?" I gesture at all the medals on the wall. "Didn't you get one when you were discharged?"

"Cashed it out so I could buy the *Lady*." His expression grows hard. "Where's your pension?"

"Donated it," I say flatly. I don't want to talk about this.

"Donated? But didn't you have an honorable discharge? For valor? You could live comfortably off that for the rest of your life."

I grind my teeth. "Didn't want it." Blood money. Seemed

fairer that I give it to the families whose lives I ruined rather than keep it and drink it away. I get to my feet. "We need to make this delivery, then. Provided they don't need a rescue, of course." I'm pissed. It'll be a huge pain to try to line up another job, and I'll have to eat vend-machine soup until I do, but I'll manage. I think of Niri, who's elderly and cranky. It's going to be a lot harder for her to line something else up, and I know she doesn't have a nest egg. And the captain… This ship is all he's got. I hate that I somehow feel responsible for their livelihoods. "When do we visit Farli's people, then?"

"You seem to have a rapport with her. Talk to her and have her let us know where they are located. We can fly there shortly."

I nod calmly, even though my thoughts are chaos. "I'll see what I can do."

"Very good, Vendasi."

"Mardok." I glance uneasily at the flag on the wall. Hate that thing. I see it in my dreams. More like nightmares.

The captain flicks a hand at me. "Dismissed."

CHAPTER 6

MARDOK

I'M STILL SEETHING FROM THE conversation with the captain as I head through the empty halls of the ship. He's been quiet lately, but he's not the most garrulous of men, even on a good day. I didn't think anything of it. To think that I might not have a job—hell, a home—when we're done here… More than Farli's tribe is at stake now. Niri and Trakan and Chatav will all be without a job if we don't get this delivery out. What if Farli's people do want to be rescued? Do we dump the cargo and screw ourselves out of a living, or do we tell them to wait patiently for the next rescue ship? We could alert the nearest Interplanetary Enforcement station and notify them of the situation, but that opens *The Tranquil Lady's* crew to suspicion for being in the area in the first place. They might delay us just for questioning. And if they do take charge, Farli and her people will be shuttled through the system and…I'll never see her again.

Either way, once I leave this planet, Farli is long gone. For some reason, that disturbs me far more than it should. I've just met her. I shouldn't care. Instead, I'm obsessing over her with every waking moment. And as I head toward med bay, I keep picturing how Farli's going to react when I leave. She thinks we're married. According to her customs, because she 'sang' to me, we're now together and should make babies.

It's absolutely crazy.

And yet…I'm drawn to Farli, far more than anyone I've ever met in my life. Maybe it's the fascination of her naïve happiness. She's brimming with life and love and hope and all the things I lost long ago. That has to be why I'm obsessed with her. That and the obscene way she puts her mouth on me.

It's normal, and it'll fade. A guy like me won't hold her interest. She deserves better. She certainly deserves better than a life stuck on this iceball of a remote planet. And I can't give her much of a life, on or off it. I'm just a loner with a small bank account and an even smaller living space. No family. Not many friends. If I disappeared, no one would miss me, except maybe Niri.

My thoughts are dark as med bay opens. Both Farli and Niri are still here, and Farli's ridiculous, smelly pet is in the corner, chewing on something, tail flicking. Farli's dressed in a thin plastic gown as she sits on Niri's examining table. She swings her legs like a kit, and her face lights up with excitement the moment she sees me. Even from across the room, I can hear her begin to purr. And I smile despite myself. She's like a ray of sunshine breaking through the clouds, and just seeing her delight at my return…it makes me feel too keffing good. "Sorry I took so long to return."

"I missed you," Farli says, beaming at me. In the gown, swinging her legs, she looks like a kid. But then she licks her lips and her gaze moves over me possessively, and I remember all the very adult things we did last night. She's not a child. Not in the slightest.

Niri looks up from her scanner. "Oh good. We're just finishing up here." She squints at her screen and then looks at me, then back at it again. "Huh."

"What?" I ask.

"Nothing." She taps a few buttons and then puts her pad in a pocket of her jumpsuit. "Are we done here?"

"I should take Chahm-pee outside if you do not want him dropping dung in here," Farli says as she hops to her feet and pulls the plastic gown over her head. Her gorgeous body is suddenly nude, and my mouth goes dry at the sight of all that blue skin and her long legs. My gaze is drawn to the vee between her thighs, and the sight of her delicate folds makes my cock grow hard immediately. Keffing hell.

"Farli!" Niri squawks, and rushes over with a blanket. "What are you doing?"

She gives Niri a confused look, glancing over at me. "I am not cold."

"I don't care!" She wraps Farli in the blanket. "Get dressed in here. We'll wait outside."

I let Niri usher me out of the room, and I don't correct her that I met Farli nearly naked. Niri likes protocol and order. She clearly also dislikes nudity, and the thought makes a grin sneak across my face as the door to med bay slides shut. "Don't worry, Niri," I tease her. "I've seen naked women before."

Niri shoots me a look and pulls me away from the door, her bony hand clenching my arm. "We need to talk."

"What's wrong?" Has she found something terrible in Farli's scan? I feel cold with fear. "Is she sick?"

"Actually, she's probably healthier than you and I both."

She pokes a finger in the center of my chest. "What I want to know is what's going on between the two of you."

I take a step back. "What do you mean?"

"I know you didn't sleep in the storage room last night. I came by to chat with you and you weren't there. Wanna explain that, or do I need to bring it to Chatav's attention?"

I just snort, because we both know she won't do that. Niri is trustworthy. "Nothing happened."

She crosses her arms over her chest and looks at me.

"I swear, nothing happened. We talked a little and I slept on the floor." I don't add that Farli draped herself on me and slept right next to me. "She didn't want to be alone in a strange place, that's all."

"You're full of shit," Niri tells me. "She's been asking questions about you nonstop since you left. If you have family, how I met you, what you enjoy 'hunting.'" She gives me another patient look. "She has a crush on you."

I say nothing.

"We're playing that game, are we? Okay, then. You wanted me to run tests on her?" She shoots me a cross look and then pulls her pad out of her pocket and pecks the stylus on the screen. "She's approximately twenty-five Homeworld years old. Adult. Last menstruated about three weeks ago. Blood sugars are excellent, teeth and vital signs are perfect. She's got that parasite, but other than that, everything's as it should be. Oh," she adds in an exaggerated voice, "and she started ovulating when you walked into the room. Interesting, isn't it?"

I can feel my ears growing hot. "She what?"

"Ovulated. The moment she saw you." Niri's brows go up. "I was doing a scan on her when you walked in, and boom. Egg production. And this is not the timeframe for her to regularly be ovulating. So now do you want to quit lying to me and tell me what the kef is going on?"

I rub a hand along my jaw, unsure of how much to say. Niri's the closest thing I have to a friend, but she's also prickly at best. In the end, I decide to confide in her. "She thinks I'm her mate. She said her symbiont chose me for her and that we're now mated." I tell her all about what Farli shared with me.

"Well, she's not lying to you. You have sex with that woman and you're going to get her pregnant. Didn't think you wanted to be a dad."

I didn't think I did, either. But there's something so wholesome and happy about Farli that…I don't hate the idea of making a family with her. I don't love it, yet, but I also don't hate it. Which seems even crazier to me, so I wave it off. "I've known her for a day. It's nothing."

"That so? Because she didn't ovulate around Trakan."

A hot surge of jealousy rips through me. "You keep him away from her." I don't like the thought of him hovering around her, needling her, or worse, trying to seduce her. She's far too trusting for the likes of him.

Niri shoots me a knowing look. "It's *nothing*, huh?"

I clench my jaw and glare at Niri. "Nothing happened between us, and that's all I will say." I push away from her and head back toward med bay.

"Just let me know where to send the wedding invite," she calls back mockingly.

FARLI

"YOU WANT TO VISIT MY village?" I look at the faces of Mardok's friends in surprise. I thought they did not like me.

Cap-tan nods. "It is our duty."

Oh. Well, I do not know what he means by that. "I think my chief would like to meet," I say, a little guarded. "Though I cannot speak for him." I glance over at my new mate, but his expression is impossible to read. "If I start running now, I can make it there in a few days and will be back in a hand or so with an answer."

"Run?" Cap-tan blinks at me. "Oh no, my dear, we will take you."

It is on the tip of my tongue to ask how, and then I feel foolish. They live in a flying cave. Of course they can fly to my people. I look at Mardok uncertainly, and he gives me a small nod. "How long does it take? To fly?" I also worry if it will hurt when we land, but I feel foolish asking such a thing.

"But a few moments," Cap-tan says, and smiles at me.

I do not entirely trust that smile. But Mardok is here, and I trust him. "All right. How do we go?"

"We need you to show us the way." Cap-tan gestures behind him. "Join us on the bridge and we can begin. Your pet can stay in med bay for now."

Niri makes a strange noise.

"Farli can sit with me," the other male—the mocking one—says, and winks at me.

Mardok growls low in his throat and steps forward, putting himself between me and the other male. "She sits with me."

"Trakan is the navigator—" Cap-tan begins.

"She sits with me," Mardok repeats. I beam happily up at him, because he's being possessive over me, just like a good mate should be. I like it. I hold on to his arm, pleased.

Cap-tan stares at Mardok for a long moment. "See that she does not get in the way."

"She won't."

They talk around me as if I am not here, which is baffling,

but then Mardok puts a hand on the small of my back and I feel all warm and giddy, and I forget to be irritated. How can I be, when he is around? Everyone heads down a passage that leads into a large chamber full of lights and colors. This is the room I sat in before, to teach Mardok my language. Things flash on the walls, and it reminds me of the Elders' Cave. The others file in, moving past me, and sit on strange-looking stools with backs. Mardok touches my arm and gestures at an empty stool in the rear. I follow him, and he taps a few clicky things on the slab of shiny stone in front of him. Something rises from the floor and it looks like a stool. He indicates I should sit and moves to sit down in his own chair.

Oh, I would rather sit in his lap. I ignore the stool and move toward him, sitting on his thigh and putting my arms around his neck. "I like this much better."

He stiffens, and I hear the one called Trakan give a muffled laugh, but no one says anything. I look over at Trakan curiously, and then lean in to whisper to Mardok. "Why does he laugh? Do mated people act differently where you come from?"

Mardok just shakes his head. "Ignore him. He's an ass." His hand goes possessively to the small of my back, and I wiggle a little, because just that small touch is making my khui sing. My tail finds his and tries to wrap around it, but he flicks me away. Aww, he's shy. That's…sweet. I smile at my mate, admiring the lines of his face.

I will break him of his shyness soon enough.

"Starting engines," Trakan calls out.

"Vendasi," Cap-tan says. "Run a diagnostic on all systems before we proceed."

"Starting diagnostic," my mate says, and reaches around me to press a few clicky things. "Standby."

Swirls and squiggles move across the stone in front of

Mardok, and I watch it, fascinated. Strange pictures pop up, highlighting different portions of what looks like a smaller version of the ship. I poke at it, fascinated at how it can appear in the stone itself, and Mardok gently pulls my finger away. "Careful," he murmurs.

I shiver, because I do not know what is going on, but I love his voice when it is soft.

"Diagnostic complete," Mardok says a moment later. "All systems running at expected levels."

"Excellent," Cap-tan says. "Take us up. External display on the forward monitor, please."

"Aye, Captain," Trakan says, and the ship trembles underneath our feet. There is a distant roar, and I am reminded of the earth-shake so many seasons ago. I cling harder to Mardok's neck, frightened.

He rubs my back silently, and somehow...that makes it better. If he's not worried, then the noise must not be dangerous.

I lift my head just in time to see the wall ahead of us flash white and then disappear. Or not. It's like an image of the outdoors—so realistic and lifelike that I can practically smell the snow—appears. I gasp in wonder. It is like we are standing on a very tall hill and looking down. "How is this possible?"

"It's a visual," Mardok murmurs. "No need to be afraid."

I am not afraid; I am full of wonder. You can see everything, right down to distant herds of dvisti. It is fascinating, and the picture makes my world look so...pretty and yet distant. Then the picture changes, replaced by a new picture, this one of green and white smears cut through by delicate blue lines. I like the other view better.

"Can your little girlfriend point out where her tribe's located so I can set the coordinates?" Trakan asks, voice dry. "Or do we need to break out crayons for her so she can draw it? Or is a smoke signal more her thing?"

"She's not going to know what a topographical map is," Mardok growls at him, clearly irritated. "Don't be an ass."

"Well, then, how are we going to get there if we don't have coordinates?" Trakan retorts.

I can feel Mardok stiffen with anger under my leg. I place my hand on his chest to calm him, and speak up. "I can guide you, but I need the picture of the valley again. I can show you which way to go."

"You'll have to manually pilot it," Cap-tan says. "Will this be a problem?"

"No, sir," Trakan replies, but he sounds unhappy. The picture switches again, and it is the current valley once more. "Okay, where to?"

I get to my feet, crossing the chamber and approaching the wall with the picture on it. "I have never seen from this high up before. Give me a moment to think." I worry I will tell them the wrong thing and the others will grow upset. I do not wish to get this wrong. I want Mardok to be proud of me.

"Drop lower to the ground," Cap-tan calls out. "Give her the visual she needs."

I feel a lift under my boots, as if the floor is puffing with air, and then the picture changes. We are now close to the ground, and I can tell where we are. I know these lands. I scan the landscape, looking for familiar things, and then tap one particular rock. "Between these walls, into the next valley."

The ship moves, gliding along faster than I could ever run, and I gasp as the world speeds ahead. It is marvelous. Within the space of a breath, we are at the spot I pointed at, and so I give them the next coordinate. On and on, we glide through valley after valley, heading back toward the village at a dizzying pace. What takes me all day to run takes mere moments to swoop past. We will be at the village in a matter of moments, and the thought is incredible. I keep calling instructions out to Trakan, and he guides us along, the ship moving through valleys and past steep cliffs with more skill than the most delicate-winged scythe-beak.

Then my home valley appears. In the distance, I can see the shadow of the gorge. "There," I say, pointing at it. "We live in the canyon there."

"In a canyon?" Niri asks, speaking up for the first time. "Really?"

"Yes. We used to live in caves—"

"Of course you did," Trakan interrupts, smirking.

"Kef off," Mardok growls at him, surging to his feet.

"Enough," Cap-tan tells them, and Mardok sits once more. Trakan hunches behind his table. Cap-tan looks at me again. "Go on."

I hesitate, not understanding their reactions. Why does Mardok get angry to hear we lived in caves? Is that bad? The caves were nice and cozy, and it was easy to get outside. The gorge is quiet and sheltered from the worst of the weather, but taking Chahm-pee out on a regular basis is difficult, and the hunters must do a great deal of hauling to bring things down into the village. The humans love it, though. I am puzzled by their reactions, but I continue slowly. "We moved to the gorge when a great earth-shake destroyed our home."

Mardok shoots Trakan an angry look, and Trakan just slides lower in his seat. "Your home is fine, Farli," Mardok tells me. "You and your people are incredibly resilient to be able to make a life here on this planet."

Resilient? It is my home. It is the only place I know.

"Well, someone want to tell me how I'm supposed to pilot the *Lady* down into that gorge? Because it's not happening."

"We'll get out and walk," Cap-tan says. "Set the ship down

as close to the lip as possible. Everyone suit up and let us be on our way."

A SHORT TIME LATER, THE others are wearing thick suits that cover every inch of their skin, their bodies made bulky. Each one clips a device to their noses and wraps garments around their heads and horns to keep them warm.

I stand there in my leather tunic, a little amused at how much work it takes for them to bundle up. Not even the humans are this bad. Chahm-pee nudges my hand, eager to go outside. I do not blame him—he is hungry and did not care for the food on the ship. I did not, either. He has eaten all the roots in my bag, but I do have more back at the village. If nothing else, I can pry a few from Stay-see, who keeps a well-stocked hut full of extra foods for her strange cooking projects. "Soon," I tell him. "Be patient."

He bleats at me.

I look over at Mardok, still handsome despite his strange cold-weather leathers. He finishes buckling on his gloves and glances up at me. Our eyes meet, and my khui begins to sing, and his ears darken with a hint of embarrassment, his focus suddenly going back to his buckles. I find it charming. He is so like—and yet so different—from the males in my tribe. He looks up at me again, and the heated look he sends my way makes my pulse flutter.

Not so different from any other male in resonance, after all. *Wait until you get a khui,* I think. *Then you will know. This? This is nothing.*

They are finally ready, and the wall of the ship opens up, letting in a blast of refreshing, crisp air. I suck in a deep breath, pleased. It feels as if I have been trapped in the steamy, heated fruit cave for far too long, and the chill feels bracing. I nudge Chahm-pee to follow me and head down the ramp.

The others trail behind me, and I scan the horizon. The herds that wander near the upper valley are nowhere to be found, of course. The roar of the ship will have chased them far away. It is utterly still, and after being on the ship, it seems almost too quiet.

"What the kef is that?" Mardok snarls, and I look around, pulling out my bone knife. The others will be slow moving in their strange leathers, so I must protect them like any good hunter.

But I see nothing—no scythe-beak, no snow-cat, no sky-claw, no metlak. I turn back to him, a question in my voice. It dies when I realize he is not looking around him, but staring hard at Trakan and Cap-tan.

"Look," Trakan says, patting something belted at his hip. "Just a little precaution, that's all. We don't know that they're friendlies."

"They are mesakkah, just like us."

"And wars have been fought by mesakkah against other mesakkah. Just having blue skin doesn't make you a pal. You should know that."

Curious, I watch as Mardok's face grows cold. His expression is so awful and bleak that my heart hurts for him. What has happened? But he speaks again. "You're not shooting anyone. This is a friendly visit."

"And it's wise to be prepared," Cap-tan says, and gestures at me. "Even she is armed."

Mardok looks over at me again, his gaze on my knife. His eyes are slits, and I cannot tell what he is thinking, but it is clear to me that he is not happy. He glares at the others in his party and then moves to my side, protectively. "Lead on, Farli."

"Is all well?" I whisper to him.

"All is well," he tells me, and there's grim determination in his voice. "No one will ever harm you while I am breathing."

I chuckle, because he sounds so very determined. I love it. I open my mouth to speak, but I see something in the distance that makes me pause. It is a row of my people. They are too far away to make out most of them, but I see Pashov's one lone horn, and Raahosh's crooked ones. I see Aehako's hulking form and the tall, proud stance of my chief. They carry spears.

All hunters. All males. No one else. And they are not approaching to greet us.

Oh no.

I can imagine the panic going through their minds. The last time a ship came, it tried to take away the humans. I scan the line of them again, and I do not see the fierce Leezh next to Raahosh, which means she has been told to wait below. I bet she did not like that much. "I should go talk to them."

"Why?" Mardok asks, moving to my side. "Is everything all right?"

"They think you are the enemy. They are ready to protect their mates." I turn and put my hands on Mardok's shoulders. "Let me go and speak to my chief and reassure him that you are not here to bother us."

"I'll go with you. To protect you."

I give him a curious look, pleased that he is so protective but puzzled as to why I need protecting from my own people. "Why?"

"To show that I am not the enemy."

Because he is my mate? Thoughtful but unnecessary. "Let me ease their fears. Wait here. I will speak to them." I turn to leave, and he grabs my hand. I look back at him, surprised, and there is torment on his face.

"I don't want this to be the last time we see each other," he says, voice low.

My khui begins to sing wildly, and I smile at him. "It will not be." I squeeze his hand and then reluctantly let it go, our fingers dragging as we pull away, as if our skin is reluctant to let us part. I am relieved that he remains behind, though the look on his face is clearly mutinous. He does not want me to go. It fills me with warmth that he is feeling this despite not having a khui of his own.

Soon enough, I decide. A sa-kohtsk hunt must be done very soon.

I move forward to the line of my tribesmates, guarding the entrance to the gorge where the pulley and the rope ladder are. No one comes forward to meet me, which means they are more worried than I thought. "All is well," I say when I am close enough. "I promise. They are not here to hurt us."

Vektal rushes forward, crossing the short distance between us. He grabs my arm and drags me back toward the hunters. "Farli, what is going on?"

"It is fine, truly—"

"Hey!" snarls Mardok from behind me. "Don't you keffing touch her!"

Oh no. Two of my tribesmates advance, spears at the ready. "No, wait. It is all right!"

"Move back, Farli," my chief says. "Go stand behind the hunters. We will protect you."

"Protect me?" Has everyone gone mad? "He is my mate!"

That stops everyone in their tracks. Everyone except Mardok, that is. He rushes to my side and pulls me away from the others, tucking me behind him as if to protect me from my tribe.

The others stare. Aehako starts to grin, and Pashov smirks. Bek just rolls his eyes.

"Resonance, eh?" Vektal says, looking between me and Mardok. "I am sure there is a good story behind this. Did he travel here to resonate with you? Or is he stranded like Georgie and her people?"

"*He* has a name," Mardok says in a cold voice. "And he can understand everything you're saying."

"He and his people are like us," I tell Vektal, moving out from behind my mate and approaching. "They did not plan to be here, and when I saw the ship land, I approached it."

Vektal's eyes narrow at me. "Why would you do such a thing? You know that the other caves that landed here—"

"I know," I say quickly, putting my hands up. I can feel Mardok growing tense behind me, and I need to calm everyone down. "I stayed a safe distance away until I saw one of them come out. Then, when I saw they were sa-khui like us, I approached." I clasp my hands and place them over my heart. "And I resonated to Mardok."

My brother Pashov claps a hand over his brow and shakes his head. Someone else snorts with laughter.

"Just because they look like us does not mean they are not the enemy," Vektal tells me, a stern note in his voice. He leans forward on his spear, still displeased with me. "What would you have done if they decided they would grab you and take you away?"

I laugh, because the idea is silly. "He is not stealing me. And besides, I have a khui. I cannot leave this place. A khui cannot be removed."

CHAPTER 7

MARDOK

I KEEP MY FEATURES CAREFULLY neutral, though inside I am struggling.

I could take Farli away from here. I could tell the others it is for her own good and she deserves a shot at civilization no matter what she thinks. Better yet, I do not tell the others until we are far away from Kopan VI and then they won't have a choice about turning around. I could take her with me and seduce her with kisses and caresses until she never wants to come back here. Until she'd rather spend her time in my bed than anywhere else.

The thought fills me with intense hunger. I've never wanted anything as badly as I want Farli. And even though it's wrong to think about it, I don't care. I'm not a nice guy. Never have been, never will be. And the thought of keeping Farli—whether or not she wants to be kept—is a tempting one.

I keep that to myself, though. She thinks she is safe here.

That she cannot possibly leave this planet because of her symbiont, but I know that our med bay technology can remove it as easily as it can stitch a wound shut.

Plenty of time to convince her to go with me still.

The more I think about it, the more I like the idea. Traveling wouldn't be so lonely if I had someone like Farli with me. Someone to make me smile, to share my thoughts with, to watch light up in wonder at the sight of a ringed planet or passing by an asteroid belt that glitters with distant sunlight. I could get a freighter of my own, maybe, and she could help me crew it. Most of all, it'd be someone at my side.

Someone who also mouth-kisses like a vid actress and snuggles up against me as if I'm the thing she's wanted most in this world.

She is talking happily to her chief, and I assess the men standing before me. To a one, they look fierce and untamed. Scary keffers, that's for sure. They are dressed in loincloths, and a few wear vests strapped with knives of varying sizes. No one has capped horns, and a few of them are scarred up. To a one, they are bulky with muscle and look as if they could tear the much leaner (but taller) Trakan to bits without a second thought. I'm glad I've kept in shape since leaving the military, because I could stand toe to toe with these beasts if I had to. But it's a little intimidating to see how fierce they are.

Farli turns back to me as the others put their weapons away or relax. "Bring your people. We will have a celebration and you can meet everyone." Her smile is brilliant.

I nod. "I'll let the captain know. He should meet the chief, offer his greetings."

The intimidating one that has to be the chief nods, crossing his arms over his nearly bare chest. His eyes don't seem to have the same glowing warmth that Farli's do. Instead, they carry a warning. He might be welcoming us, but he is still uncertain of whether or not we can be trusted. I don't blame him.

I turn and head back to where Trakan, Niri and Chatav are waiting. They look cautious, but Chatav steps forward to meet me.

"I'm not even going to rebuke you on disobeying orders," he says to me. "Just tell me if they're willing to meet."

"They are."

"And the one in front is the chief?" He eyes the big one over my shoulder. "Do you know if they have a particular greeting that would not be offensive?"

I think for a moment, and my ears flush with heat as I remember how Farli greeted me—with her mouth. "I, ah, think you should just introduce yourself."

OUR TWO PARTIES MEET, AND even though things are a little awkward, soon enough we are all heading down into the gorge to check out the village. After Farli's story of living in a cave, and given that these people are carrying spears and are dressed in skins, I expect something a lot more primitive than the tiny cluster of houses and the cobblestone streets. Each dwelling is topped with a tented set of skins complete with a smoke-hole, and the walls themselves are tightly bricked. There has to be several dozen of the small houses, and one large meeting house at the far end of the village.

"You built this all yourselves?" I ask Farli, surprised. "It must have been a lot of work."

"We found it," her hovering, protective brother tells me. It is the one with one horn, and he likes to walk between myself and Farli every now and then, as if he can push us apart. Farli shoves him aside and takes my arm to put a stop to that.

"Go away, Pashov," she tells him in a cheery voice. To me, she says, "The houses were here when we came, but the people were long gone. We just put tops on them and moved in."

I glance over at Niri, but she shrugs. "Two civilizations here seems strange to me, but I'm guessing whoever did the initial survey here didn't do a very good job if they missed this."

We're led to the large meeting house, and I'm surprised at the wealth of greenery in here. I'm not expecting to see rows of small trees in baskets, their branches ripe with fruit. They line the walls of the lodge and the edge of the bright blue pool of water. Off to one side, there's a large, stone-encircled fire, and several women with small children sit around it. One tiny woman with a strange pale face and curly hair approaches the chief, and I realize this must be one of the humans that Farli mentioned that were stranded here, aliens from another primitive planet.

Gods, they are ugly. Their features are small and soft-looking, and their skin is a terrible pasty color. They look fragile and strange, their heads seeming shrunken without horns on them. I look at them and wonder how these males can be so happy with the odd creatures, but as the hunters move to the women and pick up babies, I realize that there are more of the strange-looking females than mesakkah females.

And I see that a few of the warriors in the back of the group are looking at me with unbridled jealousy. Have I stolen Farli away from them? *Good,* I think uncharitably. *She's mine.* I shouldn't feel so possessive, but I can't help it. I pull her a little closer to me.

Vektal, the chief, brings his human forward to meet us. "This is my mate, Georgie." He touches the cheek of the pale child in her arms. "My younger daughter, Vekka."

Georgie smiles at us, displaying strangely shaped teeth. "Pleased to meet all of you. Are you from the sakh homeworld or another planet?"

I am surprised at how quickly the human understands something as baffling to Farli as space travel. "Do your people have interplanetary travel, then?"

"Not quite yet. We've made it into space but not much farther than that. Humanity—the people on planet Earth, where we come from—is just now branching out in that direction." Her expression looks hesitant, and she holds the child in her arms a little closer. "You…you haven't seen people like me before, then?"

"Earth is a D-class planet, I am afraid," Captain Chatav says. "It is off limits until technology has reached acceptable levels."

She nods slowly. "Ah. Well, I don't know if that's good or bad. Good, because I would hate to think there are a million humans out there being stolen, but bad because clearly *someone's* stealing them." She grimaces. "I'm sorry, here I am going on and on about me. We just have so many questions and we can't get answers now that the Elders' Ship is toast."

"Elders' Ship?" Niri asks. "There's another ship here?"

"Salvage," Trakan murmurs in Mesakkah, rubbing his hands together.

Georgie nods. "Come sit by the fire. We're preparing food, though I admit it's not much. We weren't expecting visitors." She hands her child off to another human female, one who has several children around her. They all watch me with wary eyes. "And yes," Georgie says again. "The original ship that brought the sa-khui here to this place is still around, but it was damaged badly in the big earthquake several years ago."

The four of us are seated on hide-covered stools made of what look like long animal bones instead of wood. The fire is stoked, and it's warm enough in the meeting house that I can unzip my insulated suit without feeling as if I'm going to freeze. Niri sits next to me and leans in. "There are a lot of cross-breed children here. I didn't think the two species were compatible seeing as they're from completely different planets."

I shrug. "They seem happy." I see one great-horned savage lean down and press a kiss to the forehead of his dainty human wife, then he takes their child in his arms and swings it around. The child's laughter fills the air. Everywhere I look, these people are happy. It's strange. It doesn't matter that the planet is bitterly cold and barren and that they're living in a canyon and wearing furs. Everyone's so damned happy. It's almost as if they enjoy this primitive lifestyle.

Niri is right, though—there are a lot of small children, most of them with the delicate features or lighter coloring that indicate a human mother. Each time I look around, I see a woman with either a rounded belly, or a child on her lap. I wonder how many of the mesakkah females were left before the humans arrived. Was their small tribe dying out? I think it would be a very different story if they weren't, because everywhere I turn, the hunters seem to be paired up with humans. Interesting.

One human with a rounded figure and a motherly smile approaches us, a primitive cooking pot in her arms. "I'm going to start the food, but before I do, I should ask if you guys have any allergies. The sa-khui don't, but you guys seem a little…" Her gaze flicks to Niri's capped horns and my tattoos. "…different. Do you eat raw meat?"

Niri makes a sound of horror.

The human's eyes widen. "I'm going to think that's a 'no.' It's not something we humans are fond of either, but the sa-khui prefer their meat that way. So cooked meat, then?"

"No meat," Niri says.

"Eggs? Roots?" Her small brows draw together. "I can

make a great frittata—"

"We brought our own rations," Niri replies quickly. "It won't be necessary to feed us."

"Oh, I see." The human woman looks crestfallen.

I speak up, because I bet they never have visitors, and the human seems excited to cook for us. I feel bad. "I'd love to try the fritt-fritt—"

"Frittata." She beams. "It's a human dish. I promise you'll like it." She bustles away.

Farli passes by, and her hand goes to my shoulder. She leans in. "Stay-see is a good cook," she murmurs, lips brushing against the edge of my ear. "And you have made her very happy today."

I am more interested in making Farli happy, but I nod. I watch her as she saunters away again, her tail swishing. She moves toward an elderly couple dressed in furs and embraces them, talking and laughing. These must be her parents. Her animal is in one corner of the meeting house, chewing happily on a pile of roots.

There's an overwhelming amount of people around us, and for space-faring loners who don't see others for months on end, it almost feels like too much. We're handed babies, introduced to everyone, and many of the tribe take a turn coming to sit by us. Farli's father offers a skin of a fermented drink that Trakan exclaims over, which makes the tribe very happy. Chatav talks quietly with their chief, the human mate with the curly hair hovering nearby. Niri sips a cup of tea and doesn't eat, and so that leaves me to taste all of the dishes Stay-see and the others are pushing in my direction. I try to ignore the textures and where the foods might come from. I don't want to know. The flavors are incredible, though, and I think my surprise shows on my face, because Stay-see giggles every time I take a bite.

"Told you that you'd like it."

"I do," I say, shoving another spoonful of frittata into my mouth. It's delicious, and if I don't think about the fact that it comes from eggs, I love it. These people don't use eating sticks, only spoons, so it's a little bit of a challenge. The humans do seem to be fairly advanced, and don't blink an eye with our talk of ships and interstellar travel. They nod knowingly when Chatav mentions that we are a freighter, and ask questions about trading posts near here or where the closest space station is.

As I eat, one female with a huge stomach comes and sits next to me. She is one of the smallest of the humans, and she has a baby on her hip, one in her belly, and a little boy with small horns and big, glowing blue eyes is clinging to her leg. He watches me with a wary expression. "Hi there," the woman gushes happily. "You must be Farli's new mate. I heard Haeden mention it and thought I'd come over and say hi. I'm Josie." She sticks her hand out, and I realize humans have an extra finger. Ugh.

I take her hand anyhow, just to be polite, and clasp it in greeting. "I am Bron Mardok Vendasi, and I am honored to make your acquaintance."

Her eyes widen. "So polite."

"Isn't he?" A yellow-haired human sits down next to her, grinning at me. "That's different. I almost expected you to beat your chest and declare Farli yours. Maybe grab her by her hair and take her off to your lair, caveman-style."

I'm…not sure if I'm being insulted. "Hello," I say slowly.

Josie waves a hand. "That's just Liz. Pay her no mind." Josie jiggles her baby and then leans in a little. "Can I ask you something? Liz and I have a bet."

"A bet?" Now I am curious. "What of?"

Instead of answering me, Josie touches her son's cheek.

"Joden, why don't you go find Daddy, okay?" She smiles at him encouragingly and waits for him to scamper off. When he's gone, she turns back to me, the look on her face calculating. "It's about...anatomy."

I choke on the mouthful of frittata.

The humans just laugh. Josie waits until I finish swallowing and then rushes on with her question, breathless. "We want to know what the spur is for."

It's just as bad as I thought. "Pardon?" I wheeze.

"The spur. It's not a human thing. We want to know the purpose of it."

"Biologically," Liz adds. "We can't figure it out."

I look over at Niri, but she is deliberately ignoring me, turned in the other direction and feigning interest in what Trakan is saying. I'm pretty sure she's smirking, though.

I feel trapped. I set down my plate of food and rub my jaw, trying to think of the best way to put it. Be blunt with the humans? Avoid the question? Am I offending someone if I tell them the truth? I don't know how these people react, because their culture is completely different than mine. The last thing I want is some angry husband coming to beat the shit out of me because I talked anatomy with his wife.

"Come on," Josie says when I hesitate. Her tone turns wheedling. "You're our only chance to find out the truth."

"Yeah, if I talk to my mate about it, all I hear is about how it's to pleasure me." Liz rolls her eyes. "I doubt that's the actual biological purpose of it, but I let him roll with that ego-stroking explanation."

"I...ah..."

Josie leans forward and pats my knee. "Don't be shy. Spit it out."

"Pheromones," Niri says, saving me from an awkward explanation. "It's a primitive biological way of marking a female as belonging to a particular male. The spur secretes twice the pheromones that the rest of the body does."

"And deposits them along the hooha. I gotcha." Liz tilts her head. "That makes sense."

But Josie frowns. "It doesn't have anything to do with the sa-khui lack of a clitoris?"

"Clitoris?" Niri asks. "What is that?"

"Humans have a nub between their labial folds," Josie begins. "It—"

I get to my feet, feeling uncomfortable. "I think I will just go thank Stay-see for her excellent food."

"Sure, run away, chicken," Liz calls out as I head away. She's laughing. I don't care that she's amused and I'm not sticking around to ask what a 'chicken' is. I'm not staying around for a female anatomy lesson. That's Niri's field of expertise, not mine. I'm the one that's good with engines and computers... both of which are completely useless talents on this planet. I glance around, and while most of the tribe is clustered near the fire, listening to a story Trakan is telling (very loudly and very drunkenly), there are a few around the edges, busy sharpening spears or scraping skins as they listen. Stay-see and another female bustle around, feeding everyone, and a few others are watching several children at once. One human female with brown skin is busy watering the trees. They are a busy people, even on a day like this.

And I would have nothing to offer. It's just another sign that points to the fact that Farli should come with me. Not that I've seriously entertained the thought of staying here. Ever. It's an uncomfortable, chilly place, and now that I've stepped away from the fire, I can feel the cold seeping back into my bones. I re-fasten the front of my suit and hand my plate off to Stay-see, thanking her for the food.

As I do, I see another human female, this one standing

apart from the others. Her hair is a strange orangey-red, her bleached skin dotted with spots. She holds a small boy's hand, and there's something distressing about her. The other females are small but healthy. This one is…not. Her eyes are sunken and her arms are very thin. Her belly is enormous, and she looks sickly. Her gaze meets mine, and I notice that her eyes are a much paler blue than Farli's vibrant ones.

She's dying, I realize. Fading away.

Her mouth curves in a gentle smile of greeting to me. A moment later, her eyes flutter, and she sags, then collapses to the ground.

I rush forward.

"Mama?" says the boy.

"Har-loh!" bellows a male. "No!"

I make it to her side before anyone else—maybe because I was watching her. The female is cold to the touch, her skin clammy. Her eyes flutter but remain closed. She feels light in my arms, too light compared to Farli's strength.

One of the hunters rushes forward and snatches her from my arms. I think he's going to attack me, but his entire focus is on his unconscious mate. He touches her cheek, panic and love in his eyes. "Har-loh," he murmurs again. "Wake, please."

A mesakkah female comes to his side, her face solemn. She puts her hand to the orange-haired female's brow and looks unhappy. "Her khui is fading. It is too hard for her to carry her kit. It takes too much out of her."

I look over at Niri.

She meets my gaze, stony-faced. After a moment, she gives a subtle shake of her head. She doesn't want to get involved. Neither Trakan nor Chatav are speaking up, either.

Kef that.

"We have a med bay on our ship," I tell them. "We can take her there and see if it's not too late to fix whatever is ailing her."

Farli rushes to my side, hope in her eyes. "Do you think they can fix Har-loh like they did Chahm-pee?" She turns to the male and nods encouragingly. "They healed my dvisti, Rukh. And so fast. You would not think he's hurt at all."

The male—Rukh—turns his gaze to me. There is agony there. "Please." He offers his mate back to me, and I take her in my arms.

How can I refuse?

"I'll show you the way," I tell him. I cut through the happy gathering, Farli and Rukh trailing behind me. As I pass, Niri reluctantly gets to her feet and follows. The captain looks frozen, and I know why—running the med bay machines is expensive, and each of the treatments it doles out ends up using precious supplies. He's probably seeing credits go out the door at the thought of healing one of the locals, credits we don't have.

I don't care. I'm not going to sit by and watch someone die when we have the ability to save them.

Not again. Never again.

CHAPTER 8

FARLI

MY MATE HAS SUCH A kind heart.

I do not know why the others from his ship did not act the moment Har-loh collapsed, but he took action right away. He helped bring Har-loh directly to the ship itself and laid her in the same bed that Chahm-pee was healed in. This time, though, it gets sucked into the wall and all the screens light up as it runs tests. I can tell Rukh is panicking, so I pat his arm and try to keep him calm as Mardok explains what the machines are doing.

We all knew Har-loh was struggling and that her khui is not as strong as most. We knew the pregnancy was hard on her. I just did not realize how hard. Looking at Rukh's devastated face, though, I think he knew she was not well. I see sadness but not surprise.

The thin healer of Mardok's small tribe, Niri, eventually enters med bay and shoos us all out. We are just in her way, she says, and closes the door on us. Then it is just myself,

Mardok, and Rukh. Mardok takes us to the dining hall and gives us bland food and funny-tasting water. I try to eat to be polite, but Rukh just stares ahead at nothing. I hope his little Rukhar is not crying. Jo-see will try to keep him occupied. She is good with the kits.

Time passes, and Mardok sits down next to me. He looks stressed, my mate. The lines of his face seem to be deeper and sadder than ever. I take his hand in mine, and he holds on to me tightly. It is like he needs comforting, too. So I put my head on his shoulder and let my fingers run up and down his arm. Just a light touch, just to let him know I am here, at his side.

Niri comes in a short time later. Rukh jumps to his feet, his big body trembling with worry. "How is my mate?" he asks.

"She's weak," Niri says in that flat, unfriendly voice of hers. I wonder how someone so impatient with people can be a healer, but I suppose not all that are called are kind and gentle like Maylak. "She has a very large malignant mass in her brain that is pressing against her frontal lobe, and it looks like it's been there for a while. I take it humans aren't technologically advanced enough to remove it?"

I am surprised to hear such a thing, but Rukh only nods. "She said it has been there a long time, and the khui keeps it at bay."

"Well, it's failing," Niri tells him bluntly. "Do you want me to remove it? The mass? I can do it, but…" She looks over at Mardok.

I look at him, too. I do not understand. If we can save her, why do we not do it?

"But it'll be expensive and the captain won't like it?" Mardok's voice is bitter. "I don't care. Dock my pay. Just save her. I can't believe you even have to keffing ask, Niri."

"I don't work for you. I work for Chatav," she retorts. "But I'll do it as long as her husband signs a release that this is what his woman wants."

"Anything," Rukh says tightly.

Niri nods. "Come with me, then. I'll show you where to input your signature."

They leave, and then it is just me and Mardok. "I do not understand," I tell him softly. "Why did she hesitate?"

He just shakes his head. "It's complicated. Too much worry over money and job security. It's what happens when you get rescued by four loners." The smile he gives me is faint. "None of us are very good at being compassionate."

I think he is very compassionate, but it is clear he is troubled, so I do not press the matter. There will be time enough to discuss it later. "As long as your heart is good, it does not matter."

"My heart is not good," he says. He turns and cups my face in his hands, his strange, pale eyes wild. "Most of the time I'm just…tired. Existing. But around you, I want to be better. I want to be more than what I am. Is it crazy to be this addicted to someone I just met?"

"It is resonance," I tell him happily.

"Even without a khui?"

I shrug. "Does it matter? You are my mate and I am yours. That is all we need." He will have a khui soon enough. I talked with my father and the other hunters while Mardok sat at the fire, and they agreed to do a sa-kohtsk hunt the moment I give the word.

He kisses me. I am surprised when his lips brush against mine—because I have always initiated our contact—but his tongue presses against the seam of my mouth, and I am lost. As my khui sings to him, we kiss, lips and tongues entwined. It is like nothing I have ever felt before, and I am always hungry for more of it, even when we break apart.

"Stay with me tonight," he murmurs. "Either here on the ship or in the village."

I nod. It is no hardship to be with him. As long as I can lie in his arms, I do not care where we are. "Of course."

He presses another hard, fervent kiss to my mouth. "Stay with me. Forever."

I kiss him back, dragging my fingertips along the stubble of his scalp. At first I thought his lack of hair strange, but I find the feel of it against my skin arousing. "Always. We are mated. You will get a khui, and then you will resonate to me and all will be as it should. You can move into my house with me. It is small but pleasant."

Mardok pulls back, his delicious, fascinating mouth flattening. "I want you to come with me."

"With you? Where?" Surely we cannot leave now, not with Har-loh in med bay—

He shakes his head. "I mean when we leave here. Come with me. Leave this planet behind." His fingers twine in my mane, and he presses more light, dizzying kisses to my face. "Be at my side, always."

"I cannot leave," I tell him softly. He does not yet understand how a khui works, it seems. "I was given my khui many, many years ago. Once a khui is placed inside someone, it cannot be removed. If I take it out, I will die. If I leave, it will die. I must remain on my world."

He presses his mouth along my jawline and then moves to nip my ear. I gasp, because when his teeth brush over my lobe, it sends sensations skittering through my body and distracts me from his next words. "We can remove it."

It takes a moment for me to realize what he is saying. I pull back, gazing up at him, surprised. "What do you mean, you can remove it?"

"The med bay. It can remove it, easily. You can have it taken out, and then you can come with me." He grins as if this is a wonderful thing. "Don't you want to see the stars? Other worlds? There are some that are so warm and pleasant that it's like being wrapped in a blanket. There are worlds where there is no such thing as snow. And beaches as far as the eye can see. I bet you'd love beaches."

I shake my head, pulling away from him. I take a few steps, because I need time to think. "You would take my khui out of me?"

"It can be done. I promise you wouldn't feel a thing."

"But…" I touch my chest, where it is singing even now. "It is what connects us. It is what makes us mates. If I remove it, we are just…two people who do not resonate."

"You just said it doesn't matter, Farli. That as long as we choose each other, that is all we need." Mardok approaches me, puts his hand over mine, where I have it pressed over my heart. "I don't care if you have this or not. I don't care if you never sing another note. What you and I have feels special. It feels right. And I want to be with you. Not just for a day or two while I'm here on this planet. For good. Forever."

My heart feels as if it has been clawed to shreds. *What you and I have feels special.* But…what if my khui is removed and it feels like nothing? Terror lances through me at the thought. Remove it? Lose my bond to him? But if I don't…he will only be here for days. "You could stay," I say softly. "Stay with me."

He blanches.

I hurt, deep down in my soul. "Oh."

"It's not you, Farli. It's…me." He glances around, as if he can see outdoors. "I can't be left behind. I can't. Not here. It's so keffing cold that it makes me feel numb. The suns barely come out. And your people have little to no technology. I'm a mechanic—what would I do? I bring nothing to the table, no skills of value."

"I do not care," I cry out, my heart breaking. "You can still be my mate. I can teach you to hunt."

Mardok looks sad. "If I stay here, I leave behind everyone and everything I have ever known."

"If I go with you, I do the same."

We are both silent. He will not stay and I…I am not sure I want to go.

MARDOK

The human Harlow will live.

That's about the only good thing to come out of the afternoon. Niri finishes her work late in the day, and by that time, several of the tribe have arrived. Vektal and his wife are closeted with Chatav, and Trakan has made friends with a pair of hunters called Bek and Vaza. Two humans named Maddie and Lila have brought Rukhar to visit his mother, and Rukh has not left his mate's side. Harlow looks better post-surgery, though a long strip of her orangey hair has been shaved away. She sleeps, with her family watching over her.

Farli has not spoken to me. Not since I suggested removing her khui. I had no idea she viewed it as an integral part of her life. I guess I'm still struggling to see it as anything other than a handy parasite. But to her, it has created a bond between us, and if she has it removed, we lose that bond. She doesn't want to lose it.

I…I don't want to lose her.

We're at an impasse. I tell myself maybe I should consider staying here on the ice planet, but the thought makes me shudder. Left behind? Watch the ship depart, knowing I've been abandoned for good? The thought makes me sick in my gut. Staying here is a one-way ticket. There will be no rescue, not ever. I would be here for the rest of my life, eating meat and saying goodbye to the warm sunshine of a summer day. It would change...everything.

It is my worst fear, and yet...

And yet I am obsessed with Farli. I hunger for her. I might even love her, though it's hard to say after only knowing her for a day, but is it enough to turn my back on everything I have ever known and embrace a primitive life? I don't know if I am that man.

More than anything, I hate that I've hurt her.

Even now, I am drawn to her. She sits with the two human females. They stare at each other and their hands gesture, and after a moment, I realize it is a primitive sort of signal language that they all know. I approach, unable to stay away. "Do you need anything?"

The blonde one looks to her darker-haired sister and makes gestures. When she gets a response, she shakes her head. "We're fine."

Farli is silent. She will not look at me. I feel as if I have somehow betrayed her trust, and it does not sit well with me. Already I miss her cheery smiles and boundless joy. She should not be sad. Not ever.

"I, ah, noticed you gesturing," I say to the blonde sister. "Is it a signal language of a kind? Do you need a language file to learn to speak Old Sakh? That's what Farli and the others speak."

"My sister Lila is deaf," Maddie says. "We're actually waiting to talk to Niri, to see if she can help."

Oh. "Your sister cannot hear?"

The dark-haired one gestures something and smiles.

"Not a thing," her sister translates. "But she does read lips a little. And guesses a lot."

Lila smiles at me. She begins to gesture again, and Maddie translates, taking a moment between words for her sister's signing to catch up. "She wants to know if you think Niri's medical computers can fix it."

"I would imagine so. I've never met anyone that suffers from deafness." The thought of being unable to hear and struggling to survive on the planet seems like a double issue to me. I cannot imagine.

Her sister translates with a few gestures, and Lila keeps signing. "She says that it's not a problem for her. That she doesn't feel broken. But her son does not understand why Mama does not hear him. She would like to hear his voice." Maddie gives me a rueful smile. "And she says her sister is pushing her to do it, too."

"Her mate?"

"Not her mate. He likes her how she is. He is fine with whatever decision she makes. It is her life."

I nod slowly, and somehow, I feel worse. Lila's mate loves her enough to not care if she can hear him. He does not mind if she lives missing one of her senses, if that is what she chooses. And yet, the thought of staying behind on this planet…it fills me with an aching dread.

It's not the same as Uzocar IV, I remind myself. *It's not. I would be left behind by choice, not by mistake. It's not the same.*

But the knot of dread remains in my gut all the same. I smile faintly at the women, but my mind is in other, darker places. I'm back on Uzocar IV, with that same trapped, helpless feeling. And I can't stay here, not with Farli's sad eyes making me feel like I'm making a mistake.

I need to leave. To get a breath of fresh air. Something. Her disappointment eats at me, and I can't take it. I exit the room, escaping out into the shadowy passages of the ship.

Even here, though, I cannot escape. Vektal and his mate stand with the captain by the ship's exit hatch. The primitive chief's arms are crossed and he doesn't look pleased. His wife looks distressed, and her hand is hooked into her husband's belt, as if she's afraid of losing him, even for a second. Captain Chatav is oblivious to the mood of his audience, though. He holds a mug of his favorite drink and stands proudly, as if he's delivering a speech to soldiers. "Any of your people that wish to return with us, of course, will be given that option. Even though it is very costly, we cannot abandon a people in need on this gods-forsaken planet. I am sure we can be compensated for our time, fuel, and supply expenditures in some fashion."

"Your offer is generous," Georgie says politely as I walk past. "But I'm not sure that there is anyone willing to take you up on it. The khui would have to be removed, and the bond is an emotional one as well as a physical one. I'm not sure anyone wants to lose that. Even though we were stranded here, we're happy."

"Nonsense," Chatav says. "This planet is a deathtrap and barely habitable. There are so many other locations you could choose to colonize if you so wished."

Georgie glances at her husband, but he appears lost in thought.

"We'll think on it," she says eventually. I don't stick around to eavesdrop. I can tell just what Vektal is thinking without him saying a word. He won't leave, but it doesn't mean that he won't encourage his wife or children to seek out a better life if one is to be had. He's going to think of what's best for them and not for him.

It's what I'd do for Farli.

Or…is it? Am I being selfish in wanting her to go away with me? I just…can't picture growing old here on this planet.

Living every day huddled away from the ice and snow. Wearing leather and eating meat like a savage beast. There are better lives out there to be had. Farli would love the beach. I imagine her in a tiny swim outfit, soaking up the warm weather. I envision her taking a pleasure cruiser through the stars and showing her the sights. Wouldn't she love that? She has a sense of adventure and a hunger for new things. Staying here on this iceball of a planet limits her.

I can't be wrong in this. I can't.

I head toward my quarters, but as I do, I see Trakan and two of the hunters hanging out in the lounge. He's showing them how to run one of the electronic gaming boards, though neither hunter seems very interested. Trakan spots me and jogs out of the room into the hall. "Hey, good, I was looking for you."

I stop, though Trakan's the last person I want to see at the moment. "What is it?"

"I need the secondary remote for the game board. Have you seen it?" He rubs his hands. "I'm going to teach these boys to gamble."

I snort. "Why? They're a simple people. They don't have anything you want."

"Ah, my friend, but that's where you're wrong." His tone is smooth, too smooth. And there's a big grin on his face I don't trust. "It's about building relationships, you know? Something *you* can't judge anyone on."

I narrow my eyes at him. "What are you talking about?"

"I'm talking about the little bit of sweetness you've been keeping in your quarters. But that's fine—she's all yours. I'm working on making friendships, you know? Might be a reward for a long-lost descendant or two. Or heck, they came here on a ship. Might be able to take some salvage off their hands." He winks at me.

Rage burns in my mind. Is that all these people are to him? A money-making scheme? Is that why he's teaching them to gamble? So he can fleece them out of everything they might own that's of some value? "Leave these people alone."

"Hey, hey, don't get greedy." He puts his hands in the air. "Like I said, you've got your target, I've got mine. I'm not touching your little piece of tail—"

I slam my fist into his keffing mouth. How keffing dare he? Farli isn't a piece of 'tail.' I think of her laughing eyes and her innocent smiles. I think of Trakan taking someone like her into one of the back rooms and trying to talk circles around her to get what he wants out of her.

And as Trakan staggers backward and mutters a "What the hell?" I go after him again.

I fling myself onto him, fists flying. Trakan tries to land a few punches, but I'm the security expert on the crew, and he's just a skinny, underdeveloped navigator. He tries to block me, but I'm stronger than him, and I know where to hit. My fist slams into his brow, his mouth, and I can't stop myself. Over and over, I see Trakan in my mind, cornering Farli and trying to manipulate her. I can't stop, because the red cloud of anger over my brain doesn't allow me to think.

Farli's mine.

She's mine.

Someone's shouting in the distance, and then hands are grabbing me—extra sets of hands. I'm yanked off of Trakan and hauled backward several feet. I swing wildly despite the fact that I can no longer reach him. I'm snarling furiously, because I want to make him regret the awful things he's saying. I'm not like him. I'm not. I'm not using Farli.

I'm not.

But then she's there, at my side. Her hands go to my face, and she presses her warm, warm fingers against my cheeks.

Her eyes are full of concern and love, and I suck in a deep breath, trying to calm myself. I'm lost in that shining, glowing blue and in her touch. The thrumming sound of her khui fills the air, and I focus on it and the soft, breathless sound of her whispering my name.

My Farli.

"What is the meaning of this?" Chatav says stiffly. I reluctantly pull my gaze away from hers and see that the captain and the chief are standing in the doorway, both of them frowning in my direction. The elderly hunter, Vaza, is pulling Trakan to his feet. There's blood all over Trakan's face, and his lip is swollen. My hand throbs with a silent reminder of what I've just done.

I don't care. If they let go of me right now, I'd attack him all over again. But Farli keeps touching me, and somehow, I manage not to lunge at Trakan once more.

"Kochal?" Chatav demands, glaring at Trakan. "Speak."

"Kef if I know what's going on with him, Captain. I was just asking Vendasi here where the game board remote was and he lost his cool. Started attacking me. Think he needs a psych evaluation if you ask me." He presses his hand to his split lip and winces. "Been in space for too keffing long without a meds adjustment."

I growl low in my throat.

"It is all right," Farli murmurs, her hand stroking my shoulder. "Do not look at him, Mardok. Look at me."

"Vendasi?" Chatav asks, wanting my side of the story.

I remain silent. Everyone's staring at me, and I don't want the others to feel humiliated at the thought of Trakan trying to take advantage of them. I sure don't want to repeat what he said about Farli, because I don't ever, ever want her thinking that I would use her. So I say nothing.

"Guilty, like I said," Trakan tells everyone.

"Kochal, I somehow doubt very much that you were innocently asking for the remotes and nothing more," Chatav says to Trakan, tone cold. "That being said, I do think it wise if both of you spend some time apart. Everyone is under a lot of stress right now, and this ship isn't large enough to hold two hotheads in close quarters. I'm barring both of you from the common areas for the rest of the day. Spend your time in your quarters and think about what you've done." It sounds like he's scolding children and not grown adults.

"Come stay with me tonight," Farli says softly, stroking my cheek. "Come back to the village. You can return in the morning."

Vektal nods. "We will take Mardok with us. The other can stay here."

"Very well," Chatav says, clasping his hands behind his back. "I'm sorry you had to see this shameful display."

"They are hunters," Vektal tells him with a shrug. "Tempers run hot. It happens from time to time." He seems unconcerned, and my respect for him goes up a notch for treating us like adults. His strange glowing blue gaze focuses on me. "Do you need to see a healer?"

I flex my hand. To use med bay for something so small would be ridiculous. "I'm fine."

"Let us get your fur wraps," Farli murmurs to me. "And we'll go back down to the village. Come."

I let her lead me away, though the urge to pound my fists into Trakan's face is still overwhelming. *You've got your target, I've got mine.*

It's not the same, I tell myself. *It's not.*

CHAPTER 9

FARLI

MARDOK'S BIG BODY IS SHAKING with rage as I lead him away. I do not know what caused the fight between him and his tribesmate, but whatever it is, it is clear to me that it has hurt him at a deep level. He's silent as he puts on his layers and we go out into the snow once more. A few of my tribesmates are heading back, and we walk with Georgie and Vektal, who are also quiet. It seems that the ship has brought no one happiness except perhaps me and Har-loh's small family, because she will be better soon. Even Li-lah, who is getting her hearing returned, does not seem excited about the prospect.

It is as if all we have are more doubts and questions, and I do not know if I like it.

We use the pulley to get back down to the bottom of the gorge, and Chahm-pee prances up to me. He's clearly been waiting here for my return, and I lavish him with praise and attention as we walk back to the village. I might as well, since no one else is speaking. But then the small, neat rows of houses that make up Croatoan come into view, and I see people walking around, pausing to talk. I see the kits playing in the street, Joden and Pacy chasing a ball as Analay and Kae race after them.

It is normal. Good. The sight of it makes me feel better.

Shorshie turns to me, a bright smile on her face that does not quite meet her eyes. "Would you and Mardok like to join us for dinner tonight? I can make something, and it would be an honor to have you visit my fire."

I look at my mate, but he is far away, his expression distant. "Not tonight," I tell Shorshie. "Perhaps in the morning. I think we would not be good company."

She gives me an understanding nod and pulls her mate away. I take Mardok by the arm and lead him toward my small house on the edge of the village. Chahm-pee prances behind us, nipping at my boots playfully. He does not understand why the mood is a grave one, only that it is time to play. I move him to the house that is his stable, put food in his basket and make sure he has fresh water. I give him a quick scratch and promise to spend more time with him tomorrow.

Tonight, I must be with my mate. With my little dvisti secure for the evening, I head to my house and push aside the privacy screen over the door. "Give me a moment to start a fire," I tell Mardok, entering and heading to the fire pit.

It is dark inside, but I know my small house by feel alone, and my flint and tinder are where I left them. I make a spark quickly, dropping it onto a pile of tinder and blowing on it until it is large enough to hold its flame as I feed it dung chips. As I work, I wonder what he will think of my small house. It is not brightly lit like his is. My bed is not on a platform, but on the stone floor and is nothing more than a pile of the softest, thickest furs. I have a small alcove for my toilet, a stone counter for my cooking, and a fire pit. I have a rack for my weapons, a few stools, and colorful, woven hangings that Tee-fah-ni and Meh-gan have made for me. It is a small chamber, and very different from his. And it is important to me that he does not find it…crude.

As I work the fire, he moves around the house, gazing at my things. He moves toward the stone wall and peers at it. "Are these hieroglyphs?"

"I do not know that word."

"Stone drawings? Language?"

I shrug. "They were here before we came. Some of the walls have pictures, some do not." They do not interest me much, though a few of the humans are fascinated by them.

"Huh," he says. "If they're anything like these pictures, they're ugly creatures. Four arms and no horns."

"They are long gone," I say, and add a teasing note to my voice. "You do not have to worry about them returning to scare you out of your sleep."

He looks over at me, and a hint of a smile curves his mouth. "Guess not."

I like that his mood is lightening a bit. I stoke the fire higher, adding in even more fuel so he will not be cold. It's odd to look over and not see his eyes glowing in the darkness. *No khui*, I remind myself. Maybe never. And I grow a little sad at the thought. Just as quickly, I push it aside. If I will only have a few days with Mardok, then I will make the most of them. I will grieve and feel sorry for myself later, when his ship has disappeared from the sky and I am left empty and alone.

But for now, he is here. I will worry about everything else tomorrow. I pat the stool next to where I crouch. "Come and sit by the fire."

Mardok approaches, and I notice some of the strain is easing from his face now that we are alone. I am glad. He sits down and unbuckles the front of his suit, then rubs his hands and holds them out to the fire. "It's getting colder."

"It does get brisk when the suns go down. Do not worry—we will stay warm under the furs."

Instead of making him smile, he looks unhappy. "Farli…"

"Shhh," I tell him. "I ask nothing of you but your company while you are here. You cannot stay, and I am not sure I wish to leave." I shake my head. "It is as it has been made. All we can do is enjoy the time we have."

His eyes are still sad, but he nods. When I stand, he grabs me by the hips and tugs me into his lap. "If that's the case, then I'm not letting go of you tonight."

I chuckle and wrap my arms around his neck, because I do not mind this in the slightest. "Are you hungry? Thirsty?"

"Nope." Mardok presses a kiss to the bony plates on my shoulder. "I was cold, but I'm warmer with you in my arms."

"Shall we undress and get under the furs? You will be much warmer with your naked skin pressed against mine."

He closes his eyes and groans, pressing his forehead to the exact spot he just kissed. "Have mercy on a man."

"Why? It is practical."

"And I won't be able to resist touching you."

I snort. Is that his only worry? "Why should you resist it? I want to touch you, too."

He lifts his head. "I don't want you to feel like I'm using you."

Using me? With my khui singing a wild, needy song in my chest? With my body aching and feeling hollow a bit more every day because we haven't mated? I am already slick between my thighs, and my pulse is pounding. If he does not touch me soon, I am going to be the one using him.

The idea has merit.

But since he is reluctant, I get to my feet and stand between his legs. I undo the ties on my leather tunic and shrug it off my shoulders, leaving my torso bare. He gazes at my teats, a hungry expression on his face. I want him to touch me. I feel as if I am dying for it. And yet he does not reach for what I offer him. Does he truly think I will hate him if he touches me and then leaves me behind?

I could never hate him. Ever.

So I carefully lift one foot and pull my boot off, then the other. I toss them aside, my gaze locked with his. Can he not see how much I want him? How ready I am for him to claim me as his? I straighten and pull my leggings off next, kicking them aside until I am naked in front of him. Still he does not reach for me, though his gaze is heated and he flexes his hands as if he is dying to touch me.

Very well, I will continue to take the lead. It is not that he is shy, I know. It is that he thinks touching me might be a mistake he will regret. So I must show him otherwise. I take his hand and guide it to my teat, like I did when we first met. "Will you not touch me?"

The groan that erupts from him is pained. He jumps to his feet, and before I can ask what is wrong, his mouth is on mine and he's claiming me. I moan with pleasure as his tongue drags against my own, and he takes over, kissing me with abandon. Over and over, his lips swoop over mine, and I am breathless with delight. His arms go around me, and then my chest is mashed against his crinkly, thick tunic.

"I want to feel your skin," I whisper between kisses. "Please, Mardok. Let me touch you, too."

He picks me up in his arms, and I gasp, clinging to his neck. I did not realize he was so much taller than the males in my tribe until just now. I normally stand head to head with them, but with Mardok, I reach his chin. I...like it. It makes me feel small and dainty next to him, almost like a human. The thought makes me giggle.

"What's so funny?" he asks as he carries me over to my furs.

"I was just thinking you make me feel small in your arms, like a human."

He makes a face. "You are far more beautiful than any of those."

I sigh with pleasure. Such a simple compliment, but it makes me feel warm.

Mardok kicks open my furs and gently lays me down in them. I stretch out, feeling sensual, and am pleased when he begins to strip off his layers. "Brr. It's keffing freezing," he says as he tosses aside his thick suit. He is wearing nothing but an ultra-thin layer of a strange type of leather that outlines his body. I can see the shape of his cock and spur even through the fabric. Fascinated, I reach out to trace my fingers along his length. He closes his eyes. "You are the most distracting female I have ever met."

"I know." I cup my teats with my hands, teasing my hard nipples with my fingers. "It is because I enjoy distracting you so."

"Gods, I noticed." He pulls off his last layer of clothing in a hurry, and then he is naked in front of me.

I sit up, because I want to study him. His strange markings that go up one side of his face in perfectly drawn patterns continue all down one arm and leg, narrowly missing his groin. The other side of his body has scars on it, from thigh to shoulder, most of them small tracings of silver against blue skin. Some of his flesh looks to be a different shade than the rest of it, which is surprising. As he crawls into the furs with me, I place my hand on one patch on his belly. "Why is your skin lighter here?"

"You didn't know? It's artificial. I guess I should have said something."

"Art-ee-fish-ul?"

"Not real. It was replaced when I was injured in war. Part of my hip," he says, bringing my hand down to one taut buttock, and then moving it back to his stomach. "My belly, and my arm." He gestures, and now that he has said that, I can see a strange line along one elbow, as if his entire arm was dipped in a lighter shade of blue.

"It looks very real," I say, awed. I poke him experimentally. He chuckles. "It's part of me now. The flesh was grafted to mine, and the nerve endings all feel the same. Which, I'm guessing, doesn't mean much to you. Let's just say that I had holes in me and they fixed me up." His fingers brush a lock of mane off my face. "Do you find it strange?"

I cannot help but frown. "Why did you have holes in you?"

"War. It's...it's not a good thing. It's when..." He pauses, thinking. "Well, I guess it's when one tribe sends out their hunters to attack the other tribe's hunters."

Attack another tribe's hunters? "But why?"

"You don't like what that other tribe is doing." He shrugs.

"But are they not your kin?"

"Not always." His tone is growing remote, cold. This is part of the thing he does not like, the thing that hurts him deep inside. "It's complicated, Farli."

"Then let us save it for some other time," I tell him, and fling my arms around his neck so we can kiss some more. I bear him down to the blankets and press my teats against his bare chest. Now he feels good and warm against me, and I moan again because I like the sensation of my skin against his, our bony plates rubbing up against one another. "This is much better than before, do you not agree?"

"You're so soft," Mardok murmurs. "Funny how you're so soft and yet such a badass at the same time."

"Bad-ass?"

"Never mind. We can leave that for some other time, too."
His hand slides down to my flank and he caresses my buttock.
"I have to admit, this is a lot warmer."

"Is it not? And we can explore each other," I tell him happily. "I want to touch all of you."

He leans in and nudges my nose with his. "Farli...this is a strange question, but how much do you know about sex? Mating?"

I giggle. "Do you think I do not know what mating is?"

His chuckle feels warm against my skin. "It's not that. I mean, when I met you, you were naked. But sometimes I think you know about something and you surprise me. So just humor a guy on this, all right? I don't want to make you run away screaming if I try to touch you."

"Am I screaming with pleasure?" I ask, trailing a finger across his hard chest. "And am I running slow enough so you can catch me?"

"Woman, you are entirely too much of a tease. Be serious for a moment."

Be serious? He is already far too serious for the both of us. Besides, I like making him smile. "If you are asking where kits come from, I know already." He relaxes against me, and so I cannot help but add, "They come from the magic basket."

"Uh...what?"

"Yes," I say firmly, doing my best not to laugh. I avoid looking him in the eye as I trail my fingers up and down his abdomen. Such a nice, firm, flat abdomen. "When a khui sings to another khui, it tells the mated pair that it is time to make a magic basket. They work for many days and nights to make the basket as perfectly woven as they can, and when they are done, they put the basket out in the snow. They wait for the suns to fill the basket up with light."

"Gods help me," he whispers.

I smother my giggles, continuing in a choked voice. "Then, when the basket is full, the male sa-khui takes out his cock and fills the basket with his seed—"

"What?"

A giggle-snort escapes me, because I cannot hold it back any longer.

"Oh, I see how it is." There's laughter in Mardok's tone, and he grabs the hand I have on his chest and tugs it over my head, pinning me down to the furs. He leans in close, an amused smile on his face. "You little tease."

I flutter my lashes at him. "You do not think I believe in a magic basket?"

"I think you are a minx." He leans in closer again. "So I guess it was a dumb question, huh?"

I chuckle, wiggling under him. "There is much I do not know, but I know how to do that. I just have not practiced it myself."

"So I'm your first?" He looks proud, and I am suddenly glad I waited.

I nod. "Am I your first, too?"

A look of chagrin crosses his face. "Not...exactly. I wish you were, though." He presses a light kiss to my mouth. "Are you disappointed?"

I shake my head. "Nothing about you disappoints me. I could not have asked for anything more in a mate."

He kisses me lightly again, and I flick my tongue against his lips as he does, encouraging him to kiss me deeper. He does, and for the next while, we are lost in a tangle of tongues, our mouths mating over and over again. Heat pools in my body, focused between my thighs, and I raise my hips to rub up against him.

The feel of him is driving me wild, and I roll him onto his

back, kissing him hard before I break free. "I want to touch you everywhere. Can I?"

"Of course."

I sit back on my haunches, my tail flicking with excitement. His tail grabs mine and wraps around it, and I gasp. It feels as if he's touched me in my most intimate of spots with that small gesture. Tails have taken on quite an appeal suddenly.

"Did I distract you?" he asks, putting his hands behind his head. His body is long and lean like this, and I cannot help but admire the breadth of his shoulders and the finely muscled arms…and the way his cock juts, thrusting upright from his body.

I will play with it soon enough, I decide. "Is there anything you do not want me to do?"

He shakes his head. "I'm yours, Farli."

I like the sound of that. I lean forward and decide I will start at the top. I skim my fingers along the bristles of his shaven scalp. With his mane cut away, it makes his horns look even more prominent than usual, and I decide I like it. It is different, and I like all the changes he has that make him unique. I rub his head for a moment, and he closes his eyes with pleasure. It makes me smile, but I move on, because there is so much to explore.

I let my fingers glide up the length of his horns, moving over the shiny stuff. "What is this that covers them?"

"Metal. I guess you guys don't have it here."

How very strange. "Does it hurt to have your horns covered?"

"Not at all. It's just a trend, kind of like piercings."

"These?" I touch his earlobe, where a small ring has been pushed through the flesh. "It is just because it is pretty?"

"Most are. Some are…useful. Like the one on my cock."

I blink. Did I not look close enough? I let my gaze travel down his long, lean body and focus on his cock. Sure enough, there is a metal bump on the head of his cock. "What is that for?"

He rubs a hand over his face. "Uh, so, when I was younger, I was a bit of a ladies' man, or so I thought. I got a piercing there because it's more pleasurable for the woman."

I am suddenly fascinated. I poke the piercing there, and it feels warm to the touch, the metal heated by his skin. "It is? How?"

"Well, the female mesakkah has a knot just inside her, located on the inside wall. So if you rub against it, it feels good. If the piercing hits it, it feels really good."

"Better than normal?"

"Way better."

"Can we take it out and try it both ways?"

"No, once it's in, it's in."

So I only get him with the better-than-normal? I guess I can handle that. "And you had it pierced because it gives females more pleasure?" I beam at him. "You are so thoughtful, Mardok. Hurting yourself so you can please your partner more."

He rubs a hand over his face again and looks embarrassed. "I'm not a saint, Farli. I did it because I liked hearing the girls scream my name."

I frown, because hearing him say it like that makes me jealous. "Have a lot of females screamed your name? Do they use your full name, or just Mardok?"

"This is seriously awkward, Farli." He strokes my arm. "I haven't been with a woman in well over three years. Haven't wanted anyone to touch me. You're the first person I've wanted in forever. Does that help?"

"A little." I cannot help but pout a little, imagining him in the arms of other females. Did I say I did not mind? Clearly I was not thinking straight. I have a lump in my throat as a new, horrible thought occurs to me. "When you leave me behind, will you be seeking out other females?"

Mardok blanches. "I don't even like to think about that. I don't want anyone else but you. Not sure I could let another woman touch me."

That makes me feel better. "You should be mine and mine alone."

A smile curves his mouth again. "I agree."

I touch the piercing again, and when he gives a little shiver, I decide to skip exploring the rest of his body with my fingers and move straight to the interesting parts. I stroke his spur, fascinated by the hard stem of it. Females do not have one, and though I have seen my male tribesmates naked many times, I have never touched one here. It is hard, but a little bendy, a bit like the hard ridge along the top of my ear. He sucks in a breath when I caress it, and so I practice different touches to see which ones he likes the most. Rubbing my finger along the underside makes him practically arch off the furs. Oooh. I do it again, and his cock twitches in response. Beads of fluid appear on the head, and one begins to slide away. I catch it with a fingertip and raise it to my mouth.

"Oh kef, you just have no boundaries, do you?" His eyes are slitted with arousal, heavy-lidded and sensual.

I lick my finger. The taste is salty but pleasurable enough. "I want to taste you. Is this bad? Should I stop?"

"Don't stop. Hell no. I just…" He closes his eyes when I twirl my finger over the head of his cock again, making little shiny trails on his skin. "Where I come from, there are so many people and so many diseases that no one does much touching anymore."

"It sounds miserable." And he wants me to go with him?

"I never really thought about it until now, watching you."

"So how do you mate if you do not touch or taste each other?"

"Body gloves," he says, and I notice he's panting, just a little. "You put a thin plasfilm over your private parts and any other exposed skin before you touch one another. It prevents from sharing diseases."

That does not sound like fun. "But I like the feel of your bare skin against mine."

"I do, too." He reaches for me, caressing my thigh. "I keffing love it when you touch me."

His words fill me with a warm, glowing pleasure. I want to do more. I decide to use my full hand, gripping the hard length of his cock and giving it a little squeeze. He's thick and rigid here, the textured, plated ridging less prominent along the bottom of his shaft than the top. He groans again when I give him another squeeze, and arches his hips. I love his responses, and I want to do more. "Can I put my mouth on you?"

Mardok sucks in a breath. "Absolutely."

Pleased, I bend over him and give the head of his cock a test-lick.

"Ahh!"

I jerk upright, startled. His eyes are squeezed shut, his face drawn tight. "Mardok! Did that hurt?"

"Gods, Farli. I…I'm not sure I can handle that." He groans again and drags one of the furs over his face. "Kef, and here I thought I was experienced. The moment you put your mouth on me, I'm ready to blow."

"But I like that," I tell him, happy that I'm able to drive him wild with just a lick. I lean over once more, eager. "Can I do it again?"

His answer is muffled by the furs, but I think it is a yes.

Amused, I give him another lick and feel his entire body

shudder. Such small touches, and they eat away at his control. It is fascinating to me. I love being the one to bring him this much pleasure. Another droplet beads up on his cock, and I lick it away, then swirl my tongue over the head. It is a bit like licking an icicle, which we used to do as kits. I grip him in my hand to hold the length of him steady, and then drag my tongue over him once more. The ridges on my tongue catch on the little pierced bead near the tip, and he makes another choked sound. "I love touching you, Mardok," I breathe, and it is almost like I am telling his cock and not him, because my head is down between his thighs. "I like seeing how you respond. It makes me wet between my thighs."

Mardok's breath hisses out again. "Dirty talking, too? Gods, Farli, you are my every dream come to life."

I like that. It makes me want to do more. So I lick him again, imagining that icicle when I was a kit, and let my tongue drag up and down his length.

He snarls, and then, in a flash, he is upright in the furs. His arms go around my torso, and then he drags me down into the bedding and I am underneath him. His handsome face is beaded with sweat, and he is panting hard. "No more," he rasps. "I can't take it. I'll spill all over your pretty face."

"I would not mind," I tell him boldly. "You can do that."

"Farli, Farli, Farli," he says, and buries his face against my neck. "You filthy, gorgeous thing. I don't want to use you like that. Not yet."

I wrap my arms around him and shrug. "It is not using if we both enjoy it. I liked licking you, very much. I did not even get to lick you everywhere yet."

"You've licked me enough," he says, and presses a kiss to the side of my neck. It sends shivers through my body and an ache through my nipples. Then he lifts his head and grins at me. "Now it's my turn."

CHAPTER 10

MARDOK

I LIKE HER THIS WAY—UNDERNEATH me and naked. I grin down at her, and she smiles brightly back up at me, just as eager for her turn as I was for mine. I love that there's not a hint of shyness in Farli. She'll put her mouth on my cock and prance around nude just because it makes her happy. She doesn't care what anyone else thinks. There's a freedom to her that makes me envious, even as it shocks me, just a little. When did I—the jaded, world-weary ex-soldier—become the prude? Yet I can't be as free as Farli. It's hard to wrap my brain around it.

But I want to please her like she's pleased me. Except...I want to make her come. I need to make her come. I can't, because I'll blow my load all over that gorgeous dark blue skin of hers in an instant if she puts her mouth on me again, and I need to see to her needs first. I can't wait to give her the same treatment, to put my tongue on her and watch her come undone.

It's clear she can't wait, either. She's squirming underneath me, utterly impatient, and my heart skips a beat at how beautiful and eager she is.

How did someone like me ever deserve such a gift? I'm nobody—a washed-out failure of a soldier who scrapes by getting my hands greasy on a long-haul freighter. It's a job that few want because no one likes being away from family and friends for so long. I never cared, and after my father's death, I felt even more remote than ever.

But that was before I met Farli. I imagine someone like her waiting at home for me…and I can't imagine how anyone could do this job. I'd be insane to leave her side for a moment.

Then stay, the little voice whispers in my ear. *Stay with her forever.*

I'd be left behind. The thought fills me with unholy terror and a gnawing dread. The thought of watching the *Lady* fly away without me on it makes me want to vomit.

"I am here," Farli says, breaking through my dark thoughts. Her fingers caress my cheek. "You are safe with me."

I press my face into her hand, kissing it. "Sorry. I just… went to a bad place. Got distracted."

"It is all right." Her voice is gentle and soothing like rain, and her touch makes me feel instantly better. "Do you need a moment to yourself? I can leave."

Leave? While I have her under me, naked and aroused? Kef no. My brain can just get in gear, because this is an opportunity not to be wasted. I kiss her palm again, and as I hold her wrist, I begin to kiss down her arm. I'll let this be my answer.

Her eyes are bright with a mixture of amusement and desire.

"Lie back," I tell her, and she obeys immediately. Her thick hair spills out from behind the curl of her horns, and it makes her look wild and untamed. I love that about her, how free she is. And it makes me sad even as it arouses me, because taking her back to the Homeworld? They'd tame the wildness out of her. Make her like everyone else.

I hate the thought of that.

Before my thoughts can grow dark again, I kiss the soft inside of her elbow and then continue forward. I must stay focused, and right now, my mission is to make Farli come. She's quiet as I kiss my way toward her shoulder, and then I'm near her delectable neck again. I brush a stray lock of hair aside and lean in to kiss her soft throat. She makes a noise then, a little sigh of pleasure. All right, the arm isn't doing it for her, I admit ruefully to myself. Perhaps my bed skills aren't as great as I think they are. Or maybe Farli just isn't into pretending to appease my ego. I prefer that—I want to know when I'm pleasing her and when I'm not. I press another kiss to her neck and let my tongue drag along her collarbones. That earns me an inhaled breath and a squirm. Excellent.

I continue to kiss her neck, moving up to her ear because I know she likes that, too. My hand moves to her breast, and I cup the dainty, firm globe of it. The humans had large, prominent endowments up front, but I like Farli's compact, lean form. She's just big enough for a handful, and that's perfect. My thumb grazes over her hard nipple, and she gasps, arching into my hand.

"Tell me if I do something you don't like," I murmur as I nip her ear.

"I like this very much," she tells me, starting to sound breathless and excited once more.

I grin to myself and flick my tongue over her ear again, mimicking the motion with my fingers over her nipple. Within a few more licks and caresses, she's panting against me, squirming against my hand and clinging to my back. Her responsiveness is making my cock ache, and I need to pace myself or I'm going to come despite my best efforts to pleasure her first.

I slide my hand down her flat belly and begin to kiss lower on her neck, lapping at her collarbone once more before dragging my tongue lower. It feels decadent to press my mouth to her skin without protective plasfilm to cover our bodies, but after being in bed with Farli, I'm going to be ruined for all other women anyhow. When she doesn't shy away, I kiss over to one breast and then let my lips brush over her nipple.

Her gasp is loud enough to echo against the stone walls of her house.

"Oh, I like that very much," she tells me, and her hand moves toward one of my horns. She gives it a tug when I lift my head, indicating I should continue.

Heh. As if I plan on letting up anytime soon. I lower my head again and go to work on making her wild with need, using my tongue and sometimes teeth to tease, nip, and caress that hard little nipple of hers. I don't want her other breast to feel ignored, so I move over to it to give it the same treatment. All the while, Farli's little pants of excitement are making me painfully aware of how hard my cock is and how her leg is pressed up against it.

I need to make her come, and soon. Even as I let my mouth make love to her breasts, I slide my hand lower and then cup her sex, testing her reaction.

"Oooh," she breathes, and arches against my hand. "Are you going to touch my cunt?"

"I'm going to do more than just touch it," I tell her, and give her breast another lick. "Patience, woman."

"I am very patient," she tells me, and then wiggles against my hand, disproving that notion.

I can't help but grin, even as I press another kiss to her nipple. I stroke my fingers over the delicate folds of her sex... and find her hot and wet and ready.

Just like that, my resolve goes out the door. I groan and press my head against her breast, needing a moment. It would be nothing to part her thighs and sink deep inside her. Bury myself in her sweetness and claim her just like she wants to be claimed.

As I gather my composure, I realize that her khui is singing so loud that her chest is vibrating with the force of it. And I remember Niri's words. *She ovulates when you walk into the room.*

If I come inside her, there will be a baby.

And I'm leaving. I can't do that to her. I can't impregnate her and abandon her. It goes against everything that I am.

My cock can't get anywhere near her cunt. Damn it. But I want Farli to have pleasure. I want her to come, and to come hard. I just...won't. I'll hold off, take myself in hand later when I have a private moment, if I must.

And for now? My mouth will have to do.

The moment the thought occurs to me, I am excited by it. Putting my mouth on her breasts feels outrageous enough, given how stiff mesakkah society is about disease and personal cleanliness. Putting my mouth on her cunt like she did with my cock? There's nothing filthier I can think of...or more enticing. I want to know how she tastes. I want to bury my head between her thighs and push my tongue into her. I want to feel her walls tighten around me. Gods, I'm going to spill just thinking about it.

"You might be patient," I tell her, and press a kiss to her belly. "But I find that the more I touch you, the less patient I am."

"Why?" she asks breathlessly.

"Because I want to put my mouth on your cunt and taste you."

"Oh," she breathes. "I want that, too." And she parts her legs wide, a silent invitation.

I can't resist. I quickly move lower and cup her hard, firm ass in my hands, then raise her hips as if I'm about to feast at a banquet. The scent of her arousal hits me like a wall, and I groan, because I have never smelled anything more mouth-watering. I can't wait another moment, and I drag my tongue over the seam of her cunt.

Her entire body shudders, and she gasps for air. "More, Mardok."

As if I'm going to stop now. I lap at her again, pushing her folds apart with my tongue. She holds on to my horns, gripping them tight, and her tail lashes underneath her, trapped against the blankets. I grip her tail with my own and wrap around it tight, holding her against me. Locking her to me. It feels almost as intimate as my mouth on her.

But not half as tasty. I take another long, slow taste of her, letting my tongue glide between her wet folds to gather every bit of moisture.

She moans, still squirming in my grip, and I realize she wants me to go lower. That's good, because that's precisely my plan. I lick lower and find her opening as hot and wet as I've dreamed it. It's impossible to stop at this point, because the taste of her is delicious and musky and I'm drugged by the scent and feel of her in my arms. The little cries she's making are driving me wild, and I'm like a ravenous beast as I lick at her over and over again. I want more, though. More than just a few licks and tastes. So I push my tongue into her and use it like I would my cock, letting the ridges drag against her opening.

Farli's cries are frantic now, and my own body feels as if

it's about to lose control. I'm so close to the edge, and judging from the sounds she's making, she must be, too. I fuck her with my tongue, moving it as fast as I would my cock, plunging it in and out of her sweet heat. Her thighs clench against my shoulders, and she stiffens, a loud gasp escaping her. I work her harder, and I can feel her walls constrict against my tongue, and then she's coming with a little keening sound, and my tongue is flooded with the taste of her once more.

I don't stop, though. I keep lapping at her, licking up every drop of juice and wringing every ounce of the orgasm I can from her body. When she's shuddering and weak against me, I lift my head and set her hips gently back down in the furs. She's so beautiful sprawled there, damp with sweat and her eyes heavy with need.

She raises a hand to me, beckoning me to get on top of her, to mount her and claim her as my own.

Gods, I want to more than anything. But I can't do that to her. I can't make her pregnant and leave. So I take myself in hand and stroke my cock. She watches me in fascination, but when I come a moment later and spill on her belly, that fascination turns to hurt.

And I feel like the biggest keffing asshole ever. I've ruined this moment. Failed her. "I'm sorry, Farli."

Her smile immediately brightens. "It is all right, Mardok. Next time, we will make sure you are inside me before you lose your control."

She thinks I accidentally spilled too soon? Somehow, that makes me feel worse. I take my discarded undershirt and wipe my spend off her gorgeous, flat belly, and then toss it aside. Her arms are immediately around my neck, and she's pulling me against her, tail still locked with mine.

I should pull away. Let her sleep in peace. But I love the feel of her flushed skin pressed against my body, and I sink into the furs with her, my arms going around her waist.

FARLI

WHEN I WAKE UP IN the morning, it is with my khui singing a happy song, my mate in my arms, his cock pressing against my thigh. It is hard even as he sleeps, and I stroke my hand up and down his back, thinking of last night. It was not perfect, but what we had was good. Tonight it will be better, when he comes inside me. We will just have to time our mating better. Resonance makes me itchy all over, but I can ignore it for a bit longer.

As if sensing I am awake, Mardok lifts his head and gives me a sleepy smile. His eyes are still that strange, dull color that makes me sad, especially when I realize that I will never see them lit with vibrant blue.

He does not want a khui. He does not want to stay here with me.

Suddenly, I am no longer in such a good mood. An ache builds behind my breast, even when he kisses me good morning and then gets up, shivering with cold. I watch him as he straightens the metal piece he wears over his nose—his breathing tool, he told me—and pulls on his warm, puffy tunic. I sit up in the furs. "What will you do today?"

"See what the captain has in mind, I suppose. I don't think he's ready to leave until he's sure what the entire tribe wants. If there's even one person that wants to leave, we'll take them with us." He shoves his leg through the clothing and then turns to look at me, pausing. His expression is hungry as he devours me with his eyes. "I know there's still time, but…I have to ask again. Farli, go with me."

"And lose my khui?"

"You won't need it anymore." He moves back toward the bed, his leathers falling off him. He gets down on his knees and then crawls over me, all graceful, deadly beauty. I put my arms around his neck and hold him close as he presses a kiss to my mouth and his weight rests over my body. I love the feel of him like this. "Just think about it a little more, all right?"

I will think of nothing else. It would mean losing everything I know and everything I have…to go with him. Am I brave enough to do such a thing? But I nod. "I will think on it."

He grins and nuzzles my nose again. "Maybe after I check in with the captain, we can come back here and play a little more."

My heart speeds up. "I like that idea. But I should check on Chahm-pee first."

Mardok kisses me again. "We should both hurry back, then."

We mate with our mouths for a little longer and then reluctantly dress. He is wearing his thick layers by the time I pull the privacy screen back and leave my house.

The moment I do, I hear a voice call out. "They are awake!"

Oh no. I laugh as I glance over. My three brothers are hurrying toward me, spears in hand. Salukh leads the way, and Zennek has a supply pack over his shoulder. Pashov sees me and grabs me around the shoulders in a mock-choke, tucking me under his arm and ruffling my mane. "What are you three doing here?" I ask. "It's past time for you to go hunt."

"We are taking your new mate out on the trails with us," Salukh says.

"So he can meet the family," Zennek says with a grin.

"And warn him about you." Pashov ruffles my hair again.

"Warn him about me?" I laugh. "How is this?"

"We will tell him that if he mates with you, he is stuck with the biggest, smelliest beast on the planet," Salukh says in a grave voice.

Zennek nods. "Chahm-pee. And how you will not let us eat him."

I snort, escaping out of Pashov's grasp. "Because he is my pet and that makes him my family. You do not eat family, fools."

"Are you sure? You are looking meaty lately," Zennek says with a pinch to my arm. I slap his hand away, laughing, only to have Zennek grab me by my waist and twirl me around. My brothers are silly.

Mardok emerges from my house a moment later, and a moment later, there is possessive hunger written on his face. "Don't touch her!" He stalks forward and grabs me out of Zennek's arms. "She belongs to me."

Everyone goes still.

Pashov hoots with laughter.

"Do not touch her," Zennek mocks, tossing his mane and pretending to be me. "Farli is my mate." He flutters his eyelashes at me.

I roll my eyes and jab my brother with my finger. "Are you pretending to be me or him?"

Pashov grabs Zennek around the neck and ruffles his mane. "You will have to be patient with him, Mardok. Our brother is a little slow."

They all three laugh, and Mardok looks at me.

"Family," I say with a shrug of my shoulders. "These are my brothers."

"Ah." He rubs his ear, and that flustered expression crosses his face. Adorable. I sigh happily. "I am pleased to meet all of you."

"And we," Pashov announces, giving Zennek's shoulders another squeeze, "are pleased you are so possessive of our sister. She deserves the best."

"She does," Mardok agrees in a soft voice, looking over at me, and I feel my khui begin to sing again.

"Your captain is visiting the village today and staying with Vektal and Shorshie. We thought we would come and take you hunting," Salukh says, ever the serious one. "Get to know you better before you get your khui and join the family."

I bite my lip. They do not know he does not want a khui. "Perhaps—" I begin.

But Mardok surprises me by nodding. "I will go, if Farli does not mind." He looks over at me.

Mind? Mind him spending the day with my brothers? Let them treat him as if he is family? Show him the beauty of our world in the hopes it changes his mind? "Of course I do not mind."

Mardok rubs his head and then nods. "All right. What are we hunting?"

"Ah, my friend," Salukh says, handing him a spear. "The better question is, what are we *not* hunting."

A SHORT TIME LATER, MY brothers set off with Mardok. My mate has been swathed in additional furs to keep him warm, holds his spear very clumsily, and listens as my brothers talk endlessly. I smile to myself as they leave. Part of me wants to go and hunt with them, but I need to see to Chahm-pee and I need to talk with my mother. My heart is heavy with too many burdens to carry by myself. I head to my dvisti's hut and collect the dung that has frozen overnight, as well as refill his food basket and break the ice on his water bowl. Chahm-pee is happy to see me, prancing about and biting at my leathers to get my attention. I am focused on tending to him and do not notice that I have company until I turn and see Sessah and Taushen standing in the doorway.

I straighten. "What is it?"

Sessah just gives me a sulky look, his arms crossed over his chest. In a few more seasons, he will be as big and strong as his father. For now, though, he is still far too young. Pouting does not help that, either. Taushen is the one that speaks. "We heard your new mate was in the village."

"He stayed with me last night," I tell them with a nod. "But my brothers just took him hunting. If you wish to speak to him, you missed him."

Taushen looks at Sessah. When the younger hunter remains silent, Taushen sighs and gives me a faint smile. "I wished to volunteer to join in the sa-kohtsk hunt for him." He nudges Sessah. "Him, too."

Some of the tension leaves my body. To participate on the sa-kohtsk hunt of a rival means all is forgiven and you accept the loss of the female you wanted. "I am pleased."

"When is it?" Taushen asks.

What to tell them? I hesitate, then go with the truth. "It might not happen. Mardok does not like this planet and is not sure he wishes to stay behind."

The look on Sessah's young face is incredulous. "What? But you have resonated."

I know. I feel miserable at the sight of their outrage. "It is not the same with his people," I tell them. "They do not have a khui to bond them, so he does not understand. He does not like the planet, and to stay with me, he would give up everything he has." I try to smile, but it is difficult. "It is not the same as Shorshie and the others. He is not stranded here."

"But you are his mate. You will carry his kit." Sessah is frowning fiercely. His fists clench. "It is not fair that he takes the only unmated female in our tribe and then casts her aside!" Furious, he storms away.

I flinch at his words, hugging my arms to my chest. "I hate that he is so upset."

"He is young," Taushen says, moving toward me. He squeezes my arm, his expression rueful. "He has not yet learned what it is to wait. He will, though."

I sigh. "It would have been much easier if I had resonated to one of the tribe's hunters, I know. But I do not choose." And I would not choose anyone but Mardok. I love him. The moment he appeared, I knew he was mine.

"The khui chooses," Taushen agrees. He rubs my arm and then pauses. "If he does not stay and you need a father for your kit, I will be that hunter for you, Farli."

I blink in surprise. "What—"

"It does not have to be pleasure-mating, though I would take that in time. It would be enough for me to know you are cared for. You and your kit."

I feel like crying. "You are a good hunter, Taushen. You are going to make a female a very good mate someday."

His smile is sad. "Someday." He gives me a pat on the shoulder and then leaves.

My heart feels as if it is breaking. I do not want Mardok to leave. I do not want to leave with him. But what do I do? What can I do? Choking back the sob rising in my throat, I push my way out of Chahm-pee's hut and race through the village, heading toward a place I know there will be comfort.

My mother's house does not have her privacy screen up, and inside I can smell her favorite spicy tea. I give a polite scratch at the doorway to let her know I am here, and when she looks up, I fling myself inside and into her arms, sobbing.

"Oh, Farli," Kemli says, surprised. She strokes my mane and holds me close. "What is it, my sweet one?"

"Why is resonance so awful?" I weep. And then I think of

Mardok's mouth on mine, his smiles, the way he touches me. "And so wonderful, too?" It feels as if I am being torn apart by the thing I love the most.

My mother just gives a knowing chuckle. "Because it is resonance. It does not ask how your heart feels. It just chooses." She clucks and holds me close. "Come sit with me. Unburden your heart."

She sits in her furs, and I put my head in her lap, like I did when I was a kit. She strokes my hair and waits patiently. I sniff. "Resonance is not as easy as I thought it would be."

"I imagine yours is different than most," my mother says. "Your mate is a stranger. Is he kind to you?"

"He is...but he does not wish to stay." The tears start to flow again. "I want him to stay here, and he says he does not want to be left behind."

She strokes my hair again, making a soft humming noise of acknowledgment. "It is a hard place to live. Look at how much of an ordeal it was for Shorshie and her people. When they arrived, little Air-ee-aw-nuh cried for two seasons straight, remember?"

I do. Some of the humans were miserable. Only their mates and now their kits made them happy. They still talk about the weather and the cold and the lack of things they used to have on their planet. "He would be giving up a lot to stay...but am I not enough?"

"That is a question you must ask him, my kit." Her hands are soothing, and her presence calm. "Does he like anything here?"

"He likes me." I sit up suddenly, looking Kemli in the eye. "He asked me to go with him, Mother."

She is surprised. "Is such a thing possible?"

"Their machines can remove my khui. I could go with him." The idea terrifies me, because I know nothing of his world or his people, and what I have seen so far with his companions, they are not as warm and friendly as my own people.

Mother's eyes widen. "What does that mean for resonance?"

I spread my hands. "Without a khui, we have no bond other than how we feel."

"And a kit?" she asks gently.

I do not know that, either. "I am not sure what to do, Mother." I clasp her hands in mine and beg her. "Help me."

"Oh, Farli. This is not something I can decide for you." She pulls me into her arms and hugs me tight. "If it will make you happy, go with him. If it will not make you happy, stay."

"If I leave, I will never see you again," I tell her fretfully.

"And if you stay, you will never see him again." She cups my face in her hands. "Only you can decide where your path will take you."

Do I choose my mate or my family and my tribe? I have no answers. I only know that if Mardok leaves, he takes my heart with him. Will I ever be happy again if he is gone? I think of old Eklan, who grieved his mate every day until he died. How can I let my mate leave? I rest my head on my mother's shoulder, torn. How can I leave my family behind, though? My mother and my father? My brothers and their mates—and their adorable kits? My friends, both human and sa-khui? I will never see another kit join the tribe, never participate in another sa-kohtsk hunt, never celebrate another pair's resonance. I will never see Taushen and Sessah mated with kits at their hearths.

I will never see anyone ever again.

But how can I lose my mate now that I've found him? If it is truly as simple as saying yes and following him to his ship, why do I not jump at the chance? Have I not always wanted adventure? Is this not the greatest adventure to be had?

My mother smooths my mane away from my face. "If you

worry over Chahm-pee, we will take care of him. No one will eat him. He will live to a very old age and be fat and happy."

I feel my eyes fill with tears again. "You are wonderful, Mother."

"I am your mother. I will love you and honor whatever decision will make you happy." Her eyes shine with tears of her own. "Even if it takes you far, far away from me."

CHAPTER 11

MARDOK

For three days, we stay with the tribe with no answers from Vektal or his people.

Captain Chatav is growing upset at the delay. I don't blame him—every day we linger is another day that our delivery window gets a little narrower. From the sounds of it, this delivery will break him—and the crew of the *Lady*—if it's not delivered on time. He's agitated, but his soldier's code won't let him leave without an answer. Leaving someone behind would be the wrong thing to do, and Chatav is a man of his word. He won't leave until he gets a definitive response.

Niri and Trakan are restless. Niri spends most of her time at the ship, sometimes running scans on the villagers when asked and mostly keeping to herself. Trakan spends his time with the hunters and Farli's father, Borran, who is the tribe's brew-maker. Trakan's already traded a couple of trinkets for several skins of the stuff called sah-sah. He'll have to drink it before the next port, though, because I'm pretty sure it'll never pass a single quarantine law.

As for me, every day seems to be too short. There are always new faces to meet, tasks to be performed, and food to be cooked. The day is filled without a moment of time to squander, it seems. I fall into bed each night with Farli at my side, and I am exhausted.

In a strange sort of way, I enjoy it. Living on the ship doesn't allow me to be physical, so unless I spend my time at the ship's gym, I end up sitting on my ass all day. This reminds me of back when I was a soldier, working with others on a physical, sometimes menial, task. There's always a feeling of satisfaction once it's done, and the camaraderie is far more pleasant than with my cold shipmates.

The planet's still horrible, though. My face feels wind-burned and numb from the cold. I'm pretty sure I'm going to lose a toe, and I've resorted to wrapping my tail from stem to tip because it feels like waving an icicle otherwise. It's snowed every day since we arrived, and while the sa-khui aren't much bothered by it, it's harder for me to move around when it feels as if I'm frozen.

Nights are spent in Farli's bed. We haven't fully had sex yet—not yet—but we've licked and touched and explored each other for hours on end. We hold each other close each night and talk about everything and nothing. I love her mind and the way she approaches life. She hasn't asked me why I won't come inside her. I think she knows. She hasn't pressed and asked me to stay. I think she sees how miserable I am in the cold and how unhappy I'd be. So every night, I tell her about my world—the spaceports in deep space, the beaches of Homeworld, the greenery of my own planet. My time as a soldier. Heck, I even tell her about the exotic foods she could experience if she comes with me. She hasn't said yes…

…but she hasn't said no, either. I'll take that for now.

We're running out of time together, though. Chatav's antsy and told me in private last night that Vektal has until the end of tomorrow to get all the decisions from his people. We'll leave then.

It doesn't feel like enough time.

But it's what I've got, so I'm going to spend every waking minute at Farli's side and making her happy.

Like right now. We've taken a small crew to the place they call their 'Elders' Cave.' Turns out it's an enormous old spaceship turned on its side. The tribe tells me that it happened during the last big 'earth-shake,' and they made use of the computers there until then. Seems only fair that we get things going for them again, and I'm eager to get my hands on the engine, see if I can't poke around with it and make things run smoothly.

We use *The Tranquil Lady* to tow the ship back out of the gorge. When it falls back onto its side, the boom of it is deafening, and I wince, anticipating utter destruction of the equipment inside. But the tribe is pleased, especially the orange-haired human, Harlow. It seems that of all the humans, she's the one with a mechanic's mentality, and this wreck of a ship is her baby. She tells me she's tried to make equipment to help improve their lives here on Kopan VI, but she's limited by her knowledge and that of the ancient computer.

All of this makes me eager to try my hand at it, of course. Maybe that's arrogant, but I'm curious to see what I can do to help. I've got more modern equipment and an entirely different set of skills than the humans do. I know I can help out.

Maybe it's my way of apologizing for the fact that I want to take Farli away from them.

"I don't have to ride the sled," Harlow tells her mate as we disembark from the *Lady* to cross over to the Elders' Cave. "I can walk. Really."

He just growls and points at the sled, piled high with warm furs.

She sighs and takes her seat on the sled, and her mate pulls it, carrying her forward. She does look a hundred times better than when I first saw her. The painful hollowness is gone from her face, and even though she's still weak, she looks more vibrant every day. She puts her arms out, smiling, and her small son crawls onto her lap, trying to get comfortable next to her big belly. I might be taking Farli away from them—hopefully—but I've given them back Harlow. It's something.

I'm trying to justify it in my mind, I know. I can't help it. Farli walks at my side, smiling and happy, and I can't get over the feeling of guilt that I'm going to be taking her away from a people that adore her and dropping her into my world, where she'll just be another person. Another refugee in a galaxy full of refugees of one kind or another.

But I can't bear the thought of giving her up. She's mine.

As we approach the ship, I eye it speculatively. The hull is completely compromised, with gaps between metal panels and missing bolts. I'm surprised it's managed to stay together as much as it has. It's ancient, all right. I've seen vids of Old Sakh space vessels, and had a good laugh at how clunky and crude they seemed compared to the sleek modern versions. Seeing one in front of me fills me with a sense of history and wonder, and I can't wait to get inside and poke around.

Once inside, Harlow takes charge. She powers up the decrepit computer and runs a diagnostic, just like I would. Immediately, the system comes back with a ping. "Completed," Harlow says. "No errors. Huh."

Something sizzles. We both look over at one of the panels, where sparks are flying out from the metal.

"No errors, eh?" I say. "Pretty sure that's wrong. The *Lady's* computer is pretty new, and after a tump-over like that, she'd be throwing errors all over the place. Let me take a look."

"Please do," Harlow says, moving to the side.

"Rukhar, why don't we clean up in here and start a fire?" Farli says brightly. "We can get this place like it was before while your parents and my mate work." She takes the little boy by the hand and leads him deeper into the ship's main storage area. It's full of debris, most of it tossed to the far end of the bay. "I remember this place from many seasons ago. Do you? You were just a tiny kit then."

I put my hands on the input terminal for the old computer. It doesn't have an intuitive interface—where I can direct it with a few flicks of my hand or a strong, pointed thought from my cranial implant—so I'll direct it manually. I decide to start with a simple scan of all functional areas of the ship, just to see what it comes back with. "Might take me a few to get up to speed on this thing," I tell Harlow. "It's a little older than what I'm used to."

"Oh, I'm sure it's a dinosaur compared to yours," she says with a grin. "It's what, almost three hundred years out of date?"

I give her an odd look. "Three hundred? Try over a thousand."

She frowns at me, her pale brow furrowing. "It can't be. The computer's given us detailed accountings of the crash here, and it happened 286 years ago. Well, okay, that was when we first arrived, so I guess it's been…" She pauses and counts on her fingers. "Two hundred ninety-four years total. Not a thousand."

"It's been at least a thousand," I correct her. "Probably more. The language you're speaking is Old Sakh. This type of ship," I say, pointing at the terminal I stand in front of, "hasn't been in use for millennia."

Harlow seems troubled. "I know there are things that don't add up, timeline-wise. Like, how is it that the oldest of the sa-khui don't remember anything about the crash if they're so long-lived? They've been here for generations upon generations, but if I math it out, it should only be two or three generations, max. Someone should remember this being a ship and not a cave." She shakes her head. "But computers can't think for themselves, so when it tells me 286 years, I believe it. Plus, it knows human languages. Specifically, it knows human English, which has only been around for a few hundred years. So the crash couldn't have happened that long ago."

I shake my head. I think I'm starting to understand why Harlow is so convinced that the crash is more recent than it truly is. I know I'm right, though. These people have been here longer than a mere 300 years. That doesn't make sense at any level, not when I'm looking at just how ancient this ship is. I know my Sakh history. "Let's test a few things," I say when the computer comes back with another clear diagnostic.

"All right," Harlow says, and crosses her arms. "Go ahead."

"Computer, can you hear me?"

"I can. May I be of assistance?"

I glance at Harlow, then speak aloud to the computer again. "What is the current year?"

"The current year is 9,546. Day 18."

"Is that right?" Harlow wants to know.

I shrug. "We don't reckon things by Old Sakh calendars anymore. It could be. I'd have to math things out. According to the *Lady*, and by current reckoning, this is Druzhal Year 742. It's just a number." I think for a moment and continue. "Computer, tell me, what model is this ship?"

"This ship is a Szentali 16."

All right. "And how old is it?

The computer pauses for a moment, as if processing, then continues. *"This szentali is 286 years old."*

Harlow gasps.

"And how long ago did you land on Kopan VI?"

"The system malfunction that caused the captain to set the ship down occurred 286 years ago."

I nod to myself, because I'm starting to see the problem. "Do you have a history database, computer?"

"I do."

"When was the Old Sakh empire established?"

"The sakh people were the ruling government of the planet Kes. Sakh governance was established in the year 7,989."

"And the current year again?"

"9,546."

I rub my chin, thinking. "And how many years has it been between the establishment of the Sakh governance and the current year?"

"It has been 286 years."

"Son of a bitch," Harlow breathes.

I begin to type, sending commands to the computer's database, requesting different diagnostics on specific systems. "That's what I suspected. I've seen these kinds of processing loops in older systems before. There's probably corruption in the database somewhere. It can process information fine, but when it's required to calculate something, it keeps spitting out the same number—286." I crack my knuckles and then continue typing. "It'll take some time to determine where the corruption is, but that's why you're getting that answer. The computer thinks it's correct when we know it's not."

"But I don't understand," Harlow exclaims. "How is it that it picked up English if it's been crashed here for a thousand years like you said? Or longer?"

"It's entirely possible that it's been picking up distant satellite signals. That could explain how it's got more modern information than it should."

"Wow. I never thought about the computer being corrupted. It happens on Earth, too, but our technology isn't even close to what you have here." She shakes her head, amazed, then pats my arm. "Well, that answers a question that's been burning in my mind for a while. Thank you, Mardok. Too bad you're not staying. I could use someone like you to help me get this old girl running and see what we can salvage out of her."

My pleased grin slowly dies. Helping Harlow fix this old ship—or at least tinkering with her parts—would be a fun project, but I won't be here for much longer than a day or two. I'll be lucky if we even finish a single detailed diagnostic. "I'll do what I can while I'm here," I say, my tone brusque. I glance back at Farli, and she's picking up debris with little Rukhar. They're laughing, and it looks as if she's making a game of cleaning, comparing her pieces of scrap to his. She's so beautiful when she smiles, and my heart aches all over again.

She has to come with me.

"You get this slag heap up and running yet?" Trakan calls out from the doorway.

I turn, scowling in his direction. "What are you doing here?"

"Got bored on ship. Bek and Vaza went hunting. Didn't wanna go with 'em." He shrugs and heads inside, immediately turning toward one of the broken, loose panels and poking at the wiring. "Thought I'd come help out here. You fix it all up yet?"

I resist the urge to go over and slap his hand away. "This would be a very long-term project, not a short-term one. I'll help with what I can, but getting it totally functional isn't on the table."

"Mm. So it's salvage?" There's a speculative gleam in his eyes. He grins

I fight back the growl rising in my throat. So that's his angle. He's not here to help the tribe as much as he is to help himself. Salvage—especially from a ship as old as this one— would go for a pretty penny on the black market. "It's not salvage," I tell him, putting a note of warning in my voice. "The people here are still using it."

He gives me a sardonic look. "You mean the people dressed in leather skins? The ones carrying around bone spears and eating raw meat? They're using computers and a spaceship, huh?"

"Those same people," I tell him, turning back to the computer. I'm not going to dignify his comments by giving him attention. "You're not removing this ship, and that's final."

"Or what? I bet the captain would be real interested in salvage rights in exchange for our assistance." His expression is innocent.

Harlow looks worried, and anger begins to burn in the pit of my belly. Is he trying to blackmail me into silence, hoping that I'll back down? I turn away from the computer terminal, face Trakan, and crack my knuckles. Slowly. It's a reminder to him that I can brawl with the best of them, and I'm not afraid to show him my skills.

Trakan's slick smile fades a little, and he pushes away from the broken panel, trying to look casual. "Fine. Fine. You want to let these fur-wearers poke their bone tools at a priceless bit of salvage, be that way." He tilts his head, thinking, and then gestures at one of the distant broken doors that leads to another portion of the ship. "Say, can I rummage through things? Look for credit chits? If this is a shipwreck, I bet there's some lying around, and the savages don't have any use for them, do they?"

He's got a point, and it'll give him something to focus on that isn't detrimental to Harlow and her people. "Fine. Whatever. Just leave the electronics and the ship itself alone."

He gives me a mocking salute and then jogs away, heading deeper into the ship. I can hear him banging about as he crawls over piles of debris.

Harlow watches him go, then turns to me. "So, just so you know, before the earth-shake, those portions of the ship weren't exactly stable."

"Good," I growl. "Maybe he'll fall through the floor."

Harlow chuckles.

HARLOW AND I WORK ON the computer for hours. I take one terminal and she takes another, and we both work independently, occasionally calling questions out to each other. The programs and commands I know don't match up with what this machine has, so figuring out how to make things work as I want them to is a challenge. I don't even comprehend how much time is passing until Farli appears at my side with a water-skin. "Drink something. You have been at this all day, Mardok."

I take the skin and guzzle it, realizing for the first time just how thirsty I am. My stomach's growling, too. "Didn't realize it was so late."

"You have been very focused," she says, a tease in her smile. "It is good to see you so happy."

Am I happy? I guess so. The big, old ship is like a puzzle that I want to figure out, and it feels good to have a skill to put to use. When her brothers took me hunting, I was a mess. I thought I was in good shape, but the way the sa-khui effortlessly jogged through the thick snow and ran for hours, leaping over rocks and dashing over the edges of cliffs to chase prey? It told me I wasn't nearly as fit as these people, and I felt useless. This, I'm better at. "I'm sorry I spent so much time on this and not on you."

"Silly." Farli gives a little shake of her head and puts her arm around my waist. "I enjoy just being in your presence. We do not have to stare into each other's eyes every moment."

I laugh at that mental image. As I take another sip of water, I glance around and realize we are alone. "Where is everyone?"

"Mmm. Rukh made Har-loh return to the *Lady* to rest. She wanted to keep working, but he would not let her. And I believe Trakan is still digging around in the bowels of the ship. I hear noises from that direction every now and then." She shrugs and snuggles against me. "I thought I would let you keep working. You seemed to enjoy yourself."

"I want to get as much done as possible before I have to leave," I tell her, capping the water-skin and handing it back.

"Then do you wish to stay here tonight? I can build a fire and we can camp out near it."

I like the idea. There's something about this old ship that eats at my mind, and I don't want to leave it until I can get more done. Plus, the thought of being here with Farli instead of on the ship, where it feels like all eyes are paying attention to where we sleep? "Let's do it."

Her eyes light up with pleasure, and I realize I've said the right thing. This is what she wants, too. "Rukh brought back some fresh meat, and I still have some of it. It will not take long to make a fire."

So she can cook it? If this is my last night with her, on this planet, I want to try how she'd eat it. "I can do raw."

"Are you certain?"

"I'm sure I've eaten worse on a few low-end space stations.

I want to enjoy it like you do." I pull her close to me and press a kiss to her forehead. "Live like you do, even if just for a night."

"And tomorrow?" she asks in a faint voice.

I don't want to think about tomorrow. I just want to think about today. I touch her chin, tilting her head up so I can gaze into her luminous blue eyes. She's different from anyone else I've ever met, and it's strange how little time it's taken for us to become so close. I'm obsessed with her. I…don't know what I'm going to do if she doesn't go with me. "Farli—"

She throws her arms around me and kisses me, silencing my words. Fair enough. I slick my tongue against hers and devour the little moans she makes as our kiss grows deeper, more intense, more erotically charged. I love the rub of her lips against mine, the accidental scrape of our teeth as we grow too enthusiastic. Even when we kiss badly, it's still keffing amazing. I need this—and I need her—like I need air. I wrap my hand around her thick, wild hair, pinning her against me as lust drives through my body. It's not enough to claim her mouth; I need more and—

Someone coughs behind us.

Grr. I pull my mouth from Farli's soft one reluctantly and glare over at Trakan. "What?"

He gives us a dopey grin as he saunters past, a lumpy sack slung over his shoulder. "Don't mind me. Don't wanna interrupt snuggle time. I'll just be heading back to my chambers."

I put a hand out and flick my fingers toward him. "Let me see what's in the bag, first."

Trakan sighs heavily, as if I'm being completely unreasonable. He holds the bag out and gives me a cross glare, which I ignore.

"Come on," I tell him, indicating he should head out. "Time for you to go back to the ship."

"You staying out here?" He frowns. "You're not going to take anything while I'm gone, are you?" My glare silences him. "Right. Because you're so noble and brave. Big hero of the savage people. Go you. Can I have my damned bag back now?"

I pick through it, but it's small, useless junk and nothing worth worrying over. Rusted utensils and little mementos of an old age that aren't worth anything to anyone except collectors. I hand back the bag, but when he reaches for it, I prompt him, "And where did you find this stuff if anyone asks?"

"Salvaged it off a wreck floating in space. Don't know the coordinates. Pretty sure it flew into the nearest gas giant. Luckily I managed to get there just in time." He gives me a smirk. "Will that do?"

"Yeah." I release the bag. "Buy something nice for your girl back at the station."

His sneaky expression softens, and a genuine smile creases his face in what feels like the first time. "Blantah? Yeah, she deserves something nice. Gonna buy her something shiny and watch her eyes light up. That's the best thing, you know? Making your girl happy." He glances back behind me. Farli's moved off to one side and is busy making a fire. She crouches low, blowing on a tiny flame, and her features are lit up by the orange flickers. Any other girl would look ghoulish, but Farli just looks…well, she looks keffing perfect.

But then, she's always perfect in my eyes.

"She's a good girl and deserves better than a long-haul crewman," Trakan continues, and for a moment, I think he's talking about Farli. I narrow my eyes at him only to realize he's still got that faraway look on his face, thinking about his lover. "Which is why," he says, "I'm quitting."

I'm surprised to hear this. We've all been crew on the *Lady* for years now, and even though we're not close, Trakan's a fixture in my life. "You are?"

He nods. "Gonna give her the life she deserves, you know? Settle down, have a few kids, get a place. Talked to a buddy of mine and we're going to do local deliveries. Planet hops in the same system. Not much of a stretch for a navigator, but I'll be home more. This haul's my last one." He glances back at Farli again and then over to me. "Can I give you a piece of advice?"

Uh oh. "Is it going to piss me off?"

Trakan chuckles. "Nah, man. Just gonna tell you that when you find the right girl, don't let her get away. This job's just a job, you know? The moment I leave, Chatav'll have me replaced and won't give it a second thought. Won't think about it again. Niri won't give a shit. I know you won't care. It's a job, but it's not a home. My home's with my girl. I'm a big kef-up a lot of the time, but I know that me being home is going to make her happiest, and that's what I'm going to do. If you like the barbarian girl, let her know. That's all I'm saying. We're not gonna be here for much longer, and regrets are a shitty thing to sleep with at night."

"Thanks," I say dryly. I think he means well, but the advice isn't necessary. I know I want Farli with me. I just have to convince her that she needs to leave with *The Tranquil Lady* when I do. And tonight, I need to work hard on convincing her. I don't know what I'm going to say, only that I have no choice. Leaving her isn't an option. She's got to come with me. I need her.

"Yeah, well, it's just good advice, you know? I could crude it up, but I'm pretty sure you wouldn't listen." The smirk returns to his face, and he slings the bag over his shoulder. "Well, I'm heading out. I'll let Chatav know you're hanging out here tonight. Wouldn't want you to be left behind." He leaves.

And I'm frozen on the spot.

His words send a bolt of cold fear through my gut. *Left. Behind.*

CHAPTER 12

FARLI

"Mardok? What is it?"

He stands frozen in the doorway, a bleak look in his eyes. I recognize that look. He's gone to the dark place in his mind. I move to his side and gently touch his arm, letting him know I am here.

Mardok jerks in surprise, seeming to come back to himself. He shudders and then rubs his arm. "Sorry."

"All is well," I say softly. "Come sit by the fire."

He hesitates, glancing out at the moonlit snow, where Trakan is crossing over to the waiting *Lady*. The other ship is lit up with all kinds of glowing lights of different colors and seems inviting. In contrast, the Elders' Cave is dark and shadowy, the only light the fire I have made. Is it the dark that bothers him? Or is it the safety that the other ship represents?

I have to ask. "Do you wish to go back to your house on the ship? Shall I put the fire out?"

For a moment, he looks torn. Then he slowly shakes his

head. "No. I'm good. I just have to remind myself they won't leave me. They can't." But he still hesitates before pushing away from the door and moving toward the fire.

I follow him, torn between not wanting to pry and needing to know the truth. If I am to help him, I must know what bothers him. He drops to the floor by the fire, crossing his legs under him and warming his hands. I move to his side, but instead of sitting, I lean against his back, drape my arms around him, and hug him from behind. I want him to know I am here.

Mardok touches my arm and then rubs it in slow, idle motions. "I'm sorry. Sometimes my mind gets away from me."

"What is it that brings the darkness to your eyes?" I ask him. "Is it something here? On this planet?"

His hand tightens on my arm and then releases. It is almost as if he has to force himself to relax. "It's not something we should talk about."

"Why not?"

"Because it's in my past, and I need to get over it." His voice is sour. He stares into the fire, ignoring me. "It's not something I'm proud of, and you wouldn't understand if I told you."

"I understand that you're hurting," I say gently, and press a kiss to his ear. "And that perhaps talking about it will make it better or help me to understand why you struggle." I rub my nose against the bristle of short hair on his scalp, loving the scent of him and aching for him at the same time. "But if you do not want to speak of it, I will not force you."

He sighs heavily and focuses on the small fire for so long that I worry about him. "I've never told anyone…it's difficult." He rubs his mouth. "All anyone knows is that I left the military with an honorable discharge."

"And that is…bad?" I do not know what this is, but it

clearly distresses him.

"Not bad. Just not the truth. The truth is too hard to talk about."

"But the truth is what makes your heart hurt."

He squeezes my arm again. "Yeah."

"Then tell me about it," I encourage him. "Help me understand." I want to know why he is so determined not to stay on my planet. I love it here, and it hurts me that he cannot see its beauty.

Mardok is silent for a long moment again. I wait patiently, because I can feel his heart hammering in his chest. He is nervous and unhappy, and this is taking all that he has just to talk about it. I will not push. If he is not ready, he is not ready.

"I don't want you to hate me, Farli."

"I could never hate you." The thought is absurd. I press another kiss to his ear and hug him tighter. "Do you hear my khui singing to you? It knows how much I care for you. It knows how strong my love is. That is why it sings. The moment I met you, I knew you were the one for me. Whatever you tell me will not change that."

"I killed people," he says in a curiously flat voice. "When I was in the military, I killed people and I got them killed."

I go very still, because this is not what I expected. Hunters kill prey, and they do it because they must eat. "Were you hungry? Is that why you killed?"

He jerks, startled. A horrified laugh escapes him. "Gods, no. I didn't kill them to eat them, Farli. I killed them because they were the enemy. Or I thought they were the enemy."

"Because you were military," I say, trying to piece this together. My mind cannot comprehend killing a tribesmate, much less hunting them.

"It's complicated and probably very hard to explain to someone who doesn't know what war is." His sigh is heavy.

"I envy you that. But let me try to explain so you can understand. So…let's say one of your brothers decides he is going to make his own cave. He does not want to follow Vektal's leadership anymore, and he takes half of the tribe with him. What would Vektal do?"

I think for a moment. "He would be sad that the tribe is not happy and work harder to ensure the rest of our people are pleased with his leadership. It is not a fun job to be leader. He is responsible for all of us, and it weighs heavy on his heart."

"Right. Now let's say that he does not want the others to leave and will do whatever he can to force them to stay. That is what war is. People disagree and they get so angry at each other that it becomes a fight that ends in bloodshed."

I gasp. "Killing?"

"Killing, yes."

"That sounds horrible!"

"It *is* horrible. No one likes war, except for the people that don't have to experience it first hand. The chiefs make the decisions, but it is the hunters that must carry them out. And the tribes are not just ten or twenty hunters, but hundreds. Thousands. More hunters than you can possibly imagine, all fighting each other, not because they want to, but because their chiefs make them."

I feel sick to my stomach. "This sounds like a terrible thing to do." I cannot imagine a chief that does not put the well-being of his people first. "If they want to leave, why does he not let them?"

"A variety of reasons." He sounds tired, my mate. Tired and heartsick. "Sometimes it is pride. Sometimes it is not that people wish to leave, but a different reason. Maybe they look different or believe different things. Maybe they are on land that a chief wants for himself. Maybe—"

"This is awful," I tell him, stunned. "Attacking people because they look different? Killing them?"

"Or worse."

I cannot imagine worse, but judging from his grave face, there must be. I do not want to hear more of this, and yet I told him to confide in me, so I must listen. "And your chief made you hurt people? Kill people?" My poor Mardok.

He nods. "I didn't join the military because I believed in my chief's cause, though. It was just...well, a way out. My mother died with a huge pile of debt, and she wasn't married to my father. They were long separated, so due to the law, it passed on to me. I was just a kid, fresh out of mandatory schooling when I got hit with that. The only way I could pay it off was to enlist in the military, which was offering to clear personal debts for soldiers that took on high-risk positions. When you're young, you think you're invincible, so I signed up. It seemed like a good idea at the time." His expression grows distant. "There were things I liked about the military. Mostly the camaraderie and sense of brotherhood. I didn't have siblings, so it was nice to be part of something bigger. To feel like you belonged. And I liked the physical exercises and the opportunity to work with my hands. It was just... everything else."

I remain quiet, waiting to see if he continues talking.

"I was in for a few years. Managed to get by all right. Had my friends, my debts were paid, and if I didn't always like the jobs I was assigned, they didn't bother me much. Then war broke out on a colony planet—Uzocar IV. The local militia was attacking and killing everyone from Homeworld. My regiment was sent to secure the situation. That's what we did, you know? We were the high-risk group, which meant we got sent in on the dangerous shit. And most of the time, we were okay with that because our pay scale was a lot higher. This time..." He shudders.

I rub his back soothingly. Some of the things he mentions—'pay' and 'militia'—do not make sense to me, but I do
not interrupt. He needs to get this out of his head, and I do
not want to distract.

"By this time I was squad leader of my group, which meant
that I was in charge. Kind of like a chief of a hunting party,
I suppose. And right after I became leader, we received a
mission. A risky one. Our instructions were to land outside
of one of the villages, attempt to subdue the rebels, and use
it as an example to the other villagers that things could be
solved peaceably." He laughs, and the sound is hard, bitter.
"Except it didn't work out that way at all. They were waiting
for us. Maybe they had some sort of scanner that could pick
up the frequency of our ship, or maybe they just managed
to eyeball it, even though we landed a good day's hike from
their village. Whatever it was, the moment we set foot on
the soil, they attacked. I ordered my men to take cover anywhere they could—bushes, trees, whatever. It was a bad call. I
guess I was so caught up in the fact that we needed to do this
mission that I didn't stop to think about what I was sending
us into. Uzocar's not a very green planet. It's scrubby at best,
and there weren't many places to hide. Within moments, half
my men were slaughtered. Guys I laughed with, joked with,
knew about their families. Gone in a flash of laser fire. Just...
gone." He sucks in a ragged breath. "I told the rest of them
to retreat, to race back to the ship and we'd get the kef out
of there. Abort mission. Except...the ship that sent us? The
pilot got scared and retreated. Just headed back into space
to the transport ship and left us all on the surface to die." He
closes his eyes. "I see that just as clearly as yesterday. Just that
awful, sick feeling when you see your only chance taking off
the ground and leaving you behind. My men running for it,

hoping that if they get to it in time, maybe they can catch that keffing coward of a pilot. Instead, they just got mowed down." He rubs his face with a big hand. "My fault. I should have called an immediate retreat. I watched my men die right in front of me, knowing that I'd killed them with a bad call."

"It was not your fault," I say soothingly.

"Actually, it was." Mardok's voice is raw. "I made the call to land there. Then I told them to go back. Any other leader would have stuck with one decision, but I just sent them running. And I was the one that chose the pilot for the troop ship that day, even though I knew he was a coward. Funny thing, I put him in charge of piloting instead of our regular guy because he was a keffing coward and I didn't want him to break lines and cause a problem on the ground." His mouth pulls up in a hard, angry version of a smile. "Funny how a decision can haunt you like that."

"What did you do?" I ask. "How did you escape?"

"I didn't. Not really." He pats his discolored side. "Our entire squad was mowed down. I had a hole blown through my middle and my arm sheared off. I think I also got struck in the head, but I don't much remember that." He touches his temple, and I see a small, silvery scar just below one of his horns. "They must have thought I was dead, because I woke up half-buried in the pile of bodies they'd left behind on the plains."

I shiver, horrified.

"It was night. I remember that. I remember looking up at the stars and smelling the dead. There's no smell quite like it. I remember lying there, too weak to move, stuck between the rotting corpses of my friends." He closes his eyes and gives a small shake of his head. "Oddly enough, that wasn't the worst part about it. I couldn't move, but I could look up at the stars. And as I did, I saw the transport carrier overhead. They'd kept it low enough to be visible to the naked eye—I guess because of a change in maneuvers—and I remember staring up at it and feeling so abandoned. I'd been left to die." He shudders again. "Took them three days to find me. Still not sure how I lived through it." He meets my gaze and manages a small smile. "They patched me up and asked me if I wanted to continue my contract. I didn't, though. I bailed out. Got a pension, and I had it set up as a trust for the families of the guys in my squad. Didn't seem right that I take the money."

I rub his shoulder, hurting for him. "I am so sorry, Mardok."

His hand covers mine. "I think that's why I have issues with the thought of being left behind somewhere. It all goes back to that night. The moment I hear a ship taking off without me, I just panic. I think Trakan's words hit a little too close to home."

I feel sick to my stomach. He'll never stay with me, I realize. Not here. Not when it is his worst fear to be left behind. And I am full of sorrow for what he had to go through, but also heartsick for him, because I love him.

I cannot leave him.

If it means choosing between my people and the man I love, the mate I am destined to have, I pick him. I touch his face, gently turning him toward me. "I will go with you when you leave."

Mardok's eyes widen in surprise. "You will?" At my nod, his smile fades. "I didn't tell you my sad story to try and push you into the decision, Farli. I just wanted you to understand that…sometimes my head isn't in a good place."

"I know this," I tell him soothingly. I slide around and move into his lap, keeping my arms around his neck. I press my forehead to his, our horns interlocking. "I would not make you stay behind, not if it means hurting your spirit. Not when you do not like it here. I can go with you. See the worlds like you have promised."

"You want to?"

I cup his face in my hands. "More than anything, I want to be at your side. It is where I belong." I will not think about what I lose if I leave—my family, my tribe, my pet, the life I have known—I will weep for those things another time. For now, I am with Mardok, and he needs my love.

"Gods, I love you, Farli," he murmurs, his gaze searching my face. "You're sure?"

"I am sure."

He leans forward, and his mouth captures mine in a hungry kiss. I eagerly return it, pressing my body against him as our mouths meld. There is nothing for me here if Mardok leaves. Without him, I will be lost, and I suspect he will be, too. This way, we are together forever. Hungry for him, I lick at his mouth, and he groans and holds me tighter, stroking his tongue against mine. The kissing soon becomes hot and fierce, and I am panting between each crash of our mouths together. I pull away briefly, though it is difficult. I want nothing more than to kiss him for endless hours, until the moons fade and the suns return. I could spend a lifetime kissing his perfect, wonderful mouth.

And I will. But for now... "Are you hungry? Do you wish to eat?"

He nips at my mouth, sending shivers through my body. "Only hungry for one thing—you."

Such bold words make my skin tingle. My khui—already singing proudly—grows louder by the moment, the song filling my heart and my spirit as we mouth-mate once more. We somehow end up with my back on the metal floor of the ship, and Mardok's weight is pressing over me. It feels right, the crush of his hips, the feel of his chest against mine. The only thing that is missing is the matching song of his khui. A tiny bolt of sadness shoots through me, and I push it away.

I have my mate. Nothing else matters. We are still together even if we are not bound by khui or resonance. We choose to be together. Nothing more is needed.

I gasp when he slides his hand inside the front of my tunic, cupping my teat. Every time he touches me, it feels new. We have mouth-mated and pleasured each other in the furs, but he has never put his cock inside me. We always stop before; sometimes he spills on my belly, and sometimes he spills in my mouth. I enjoy it, but…I want more. "Tonight," I tell him between fierce kisses. "Tonight, I want to belong to you completely. I want you to come inside me."

"Won't there be a baby?" He searches my face, caressing my cheek. "I didn't want to make you pregnant if I was going to leave you behind, but if we are staying together…"

"Then you can come inside me."

"There are ways to prevent children, if you want," he says softly. "A plasfilm worn over the cock, or a shot of medication. Both can stop it from happening."

"Resonance sometimes takes days before a kit is conceived. It might not happen tonight. And if I leave with you…" It might not happen at all. I cannot help but ask. "Do you not want a kit?"

"Actually, I do." A grin breaks across his face. "The thought of you with my child inside you? Nothing brings me greater joy. But it's about what you want, Farli. It's your body."

I smile happily, because it is what I want, too. "I would love to make a family."

"So no plasfilm?"

The thought is unpleasant. "I want nothing between us when we mate."

The look in his eyes grows fierce. "Me either. You're mine, and I want to claim you in all ways. I have since the moment

I met you." He presses another fierce kiss to my mouth, then begins to move down my neck. His fingers tease my nipple, dragging over it and tormenting me with every brush of his skin against mine.

"More," I beg him. I tug at the seam of his heavy, thick tunic, wanting to get to the warm skin underneath. "Do you need furs? I want to be naked with you."

He shakes his head, his mouth licking a trail down to my teat. I push open his tunic, and I feel his entire body shiver in response. I am not sure if he is reacting to the cold or my touch, but it is enough to make me stop. "Mardok."

"All right, maybe we get out a few blankets." He looks rueful. "But then I get to lick you from head to toe."

"As if I would refuse!"

He grins, and then we are both racing for my pack. We traveled here on his ship, *The Tranquil Lady*, but I knew he and Har-loh would be working and that he has no khui to keep him warm, so I brought extra wraps, just in case. I am glad I did, because we shake them free and pile them near the fire, and then we are tearing at Mardok's heavy coverings. I would love to see him dressed like my people, wearing nothing but a loincloth and letting his fine chest be bared. His shoulders are so wide and appealing, and I run my hands all over the artful designs that dance over his skin. "I love the way this looks," I tell him. "It is so strange and yet beautiful."

"People decorate their bodies all the time back on my planet," he says, stripping off his tunic. "I love your beautiful bare skin, but we can get you a tattoo if you want."

I am intrigued by the idea, but I will explore that thought later. For now, the only exploring I want to do is him. I help pull off the rest of his clothing, except his boots, and then run my hands hungrily over his bared skin. I caress his chest as he tugs at my leathers, and then slide my hands down to his erect cock, toying with the fascinating piercing there. "I will finally get to experience this?"

"Absolutely," he murmurs between kisses. He pushes my leathers off my shoulders, exposing my teats, and then begins to press kisses there. I moan and cling to his horns, my tail seeking his own. His shortened one wraps onto mine tightly and squeezes, and it sends another burst of pleasure through my body.

He shivers in the cold again, and my pleasure changes to remorse. I keep forgetting that he cannot withstand the cold. "Under the blankets," I demand, and finish undressing. I slide under the blankets after him and pull him close so he can share my body heat. The old ship is protected from the wind, but not much else, and I imagine it is bitterly cold to him. "Better?"

"Always better when I'm touching you," he says, nipping at my breasts. His tongue drags over one nipple, and I whimper. "I can't wait to taste you," he tells me. "Been thinking about it all day."

"You were thinking about computers all day," I tease him.

"Between thinking about computers," he amends. "I pictured sliding between your thighs and licking you until you shudder."

I shudder now, because I love that image. He craves the taste of my juices, he has told me, and loves to lick me to climax. I am happy to let him do so, though I want more than just that tonight. "As long as you do not forget the other parts."

He chuckles and kisses lower on my belly. "Never."

I try not to wiggle as his mouth moves between my thighs. It is difficult, though. The anticipation builds inside me, and I am practically coming out of my skin by the time he kisses down my mound and parts the soft folds of my cunt. When his tongue strokes along my skin, a high-pitched sigh escapes me.

"Hush," Mardok says, and then gives me a long, thorough lick. "I'm concentrating."

"I shall be quiet," I promise, and then promptly squeal when he thrusts his tongue into my core.

"So damn wet and juicy," he groans. "Love it. Can't imagine how I've gone so long without you, without this." And he pushes his tongue into me again, teasing.

I bite my knuckles, trying to hold back the urge to rock my hips against his face. He licks and thrusts his tongue, driving me wild, until I cannot hold back. I pant his name. "Mardok. Please. I need you."

"What do you need?" he asks, and then drags his tongue through my folds again.

"You. Your cock. I want you inside me."

He lifts his head and grins at me. "I think that's the first time I've heard you demand my cock."

I squirm underneath him. "I have been waiting forever to have you inside me. I do not want to wait any longer."

The look in his dark eyes grows heated, and he glides up over me again, the weight of him pressing against the cradle of my hips. He braces one arm next to me and puts his hand to my chin, our eyes meeting. "I love you, Farli," he says again, and I am filled with the glow of happiness.

"I love you, Mardok."

He brushes his mouth lightly over mine, and I gasp because I can taste myself on his lips. "Spread your legs wider," he murmurs.

I do, and I feel the shaft of his cock drag through my folds as he rocks his hips. I moan at the delicious sensation, hungry for more of that...and just more, altogether. The head of his cock pushes against my core, and I suck in a breath, shocked at how invasive—and yet scorchingly delicious—that felt. I close my eyes, drowning in sensation.

"No," Mardok murmurs, and grabs my chin in his hand. "Open your eyes, Farli. I want you to be with me when I come inside you for the first time."

It feels as if all the air has been pushed from my lungs as I open my eyes and gaze into his heated ones. His face looks different when he is aroused—more intense, more sexual, more everything. I hold on to him as he pushes deeper inside me, stretching my body. I feel too full, and as if he can sense it, he stops.

"Let me know when you want me to go on," he tells me, and strokes my chin with his thumb. "You're so tight."

I wait a few moments, and then my impatience takes over. I rock my hips a little. "I want you to move again."

"Demanding little thing," he murmurs, and leans in to mate his mouth with mine again.

Sensation ripples through me. I feel as if I am being pierced by him, and yet when his tongue flicks against mine, I feel it deep inside. My moan of desire encourages him, and he thrusts deep, sending a sliver of discomfort through me. But he waits, his gaze locked on mine. It feels intimate and intense to gaze at each other as he is settled within me, his body covering mine. Our breaths mingle, and when I bite my lip, he rocks his hips forward.

I claw at his back, nearly coming out of my skin. "Oh!"

"That's the piercing," he tells me, and then captures my mouth in another heated kiss. "It hits you in just the right spot."

Oh, by the twin suns, it sure does. He strokes into me again, and I feel as if I'm coming undone. This is different than the intense build of sensation as when his mouth is on me. This is like striking stones to make a spark, except it is nothing but a pure blaze of heat. I whimper, clinging to him, because I do not know how to handle it. "It is too much."

"It's not," he whispers. "I've got you. Stay with me."

My eyelids flutter, and it is the most difficult thing possible to keep my gaze locked to his, but somehow I manage. I make a soft, needy noise with every pump of his cock into me, each time stroking that fire brighter and brighter. My entire body feels as if it is clenching and knotting together. He moves faster, breathing my name.

"Come for me, Farli," he tells me in a low, urgent voice. I cannot look away, pinned by his gaze, and it feels as if every bit of my body is alive with sensation. He strokes harder and faster, and I cry out, my back arching as my body stiffens. Still he thrusts into me.

I come apart with a cry, the world shaking around me. Spots dance in front of my eyes, and the breath explodes out of me. I feel as if I am as tight as a stretched-out drumskin. And still he pounds into me.

And I come again.

And again.

Over and over, it feels as if I am being driven to the edge, only to fly over once more. I do not know if it is the piercing, or resonance, or Mardok himself, only that I am out of my mind with sensation. The world is an endless cycle of thrust-and-climax.

"Your eyes," Mardok grits, and there is strain in his voice. "Give me your eyes again, Farli. I want to have you with me when I come."

It feels like the most difficult thing in the world to open my eyes again, but I do, and as he surges into me one last time, we are locked together. He comes with a shout…and I come again, too.

My breath is gone. My energy, gone. My mind? Possibly

gone. I am nothing but a boneless, happy mass crushed under Mardok's delicious weight. I wrap my arms around him and somehow find the strength (and breath) to sigh.

He pants, pressing exhausted kisses to my face. "Farli. My Farli."

"That was…" I have no words.

"Yeah," he says, dazed.

My khui's gentle song continues, the only sound other than our breathing. I thought it would stop if I were pregnant. Perhaps it did not happen, then. And tomorrow my khui will be gone. I feel a sudden sense of loss. Tomorrow I lose my khui, Chahm-pee, my family, my world—everything. I will follow Mardok to his strange, cold world, where everyone is unpleasant like Niri and Trakan. Where everyone eats bland food and people kill other people because their chiefs demand it.

Mardok will be there. I must cling to that. I will be happy with him. I know I will.

But I cannot stop the tears that flow as I bury my face in his arms.

CHAPTER 13

MARDOK

IT FEELS WRONG. ALL OF it, just wrong on every level.

I can't get over the feeling that a mistake has been made as we fly *The Tranquil Lady* back to the village. Rukh, Harlow and their small son are glad to be returning. They talk of visiting the Elders' Cave—I think in their eyes it will always be a cave and not a ship—and working on it again soon. They are excited for the future and what this means if Harlow can get the computers to work again. Her eyes are bright with excitement and she looks much healthier than before, so I am glad about that. I cannot help but notice that Farli is quiet as the *Lady* lands on the ridge just at the edge of the crevasse for the last time. She is at my side, her hands on me and a smile on her face, but silent.

I remember how she cried last night in my arms. Gods, it made me feel helpless. I think she didn't want me to know… but how could I not? Her sadness eats at me, but I'm not ready to give her up. I need her with me, at my side, for whatever the future may hold. And she wants to be with me. So why does this feel so hollow?

I squeeze her hand as the ship settles to the ground with a little bump. She looks at me, and her smile brightens. Her khui hums gently in her breast, the song barely loud enough to catch my attention.

She's not pregnant.

I don't know if I'm happy about that, or sad. *Sad,* I think, but maybe it's for the best. Maybe now's not a good time for her to get pregnant. Maybe we can be like Trakan and his girl. Find a nice space station and settle down. I can get a job fixing ships at a dock or running security. Something that won't involve me leaving her behind. But a space station seems like the wrong place to take someone as wild and free as Farli. She needs to go planetside, even though that's far more expensive than what a simple mechanic can make on his salary. I'll figure something out. I have to. She's the most important thing in the world to me.

The entire village shows up to greet us, and as we descend down the pulley, Farli flings herself off the platform and races into her mother's arms. She holds her tight and then hugs her father, then her brothers, and finally showers attention on her prancing Chompy. She seems to be on the verge of crying, keeping a desperate grin on her face as she hugs everyone again. I realize that she's trying to get it all in before she has to leave.

And the feeling of wrongness slides under my skin and won't leave. I am silent, unsure what to do or say that will make this better. I am taking Farli away from everything she knows and loves to come live with me in some tiny apartment in space, all because I cannot bear to leave her behind. She will lose her family, her khui, everything.

Getting me in exchange doesn't seem like much of a deal.

I don't have family waiting for me. My father was the last one, and he died months ago. I can't even say that I'm sad that he's gone, just filled with regret that we were never close. I can't give her a big family like the one she's leaving behind.

Farli's mother has a sad expression on her face as she hugs her daughter again and holds her close. It's as if she knows what Farli's going to say before anything is spoken. Harlow and her family are enveloped back into the tribe, showered with hugs and happy exclamations about how good Harlow looks, how healthy, and I notice that Maddie and Lila are standing close by. Lila holds her little son, and he whispers something in her ear, and she smiles.

So perhaps our visit was not all bad, then. Maybe they'll remember us with fondness instead of as just those assholes that took Farli away. Doesn't give me much comfort, though.

Chatav moves forward, and Vektal and Georgie do, too. "We cannot wait here any longer, Chief Vektal," Captain Chatav says. His posture is stiff and formal, as if meeting the most respected of dignitaries, and I admire the guy for that. However I feel about Chatav, he knows to do the right thing. "Your people have welcomed us graciously," he continues. "In exchange, we have offered to take anyone that wishes to return to civilization back with us. You said you needed time to think. Have you made your decision?"

Vektal looks at his mate, and then back at Chatav. He nods gravely. "I have spoken with each of my tribesmates in private. No one wishes to leave."

Chatav is utterly still, as if he isn't sure he's heard correctly. "Are you quite certain?"

Vektal nods. "No sa-khui wishes to leave their home, and the humans are happy here."

Chatav turns to Georgie, as if in disbelief. "Even the humans do not wish to leave? But you have not been here except for a handful of years. Surely you wish to return home?"

She shifts and moves closer to her mate, her younger child in her arms. The other clings to Vektal's leg, staring up at Chatav with big, worried eyes. As if she can sense her child's distress, Georgie puts a hand on her daughter's curls to comfort her. "There are things that I miss about Earth, I'm not going to lie. I think we can all agree that life isn't the same here that it was there. But I have a mate and children. I will not leave them behind. Humans are not accepted on your planets, save as oddities. And it would be the same at my home world. To them, aliens don't exist yet, and if I showed up with a blue husband and blue children, I'd be hidden away by the government so fast our heads would spin. We would be freaks. Here, we're normal." She looks at Vektal, and her gaze is full of love. "And we have resonance that bonds us together. I love what we have, and I wouldn't threaten it for anything. Earth might have been my home once, but this world is my home now."

"You are thinking too negatively," Chatav says in a placating tone. "If you do not wish to return to Earth, I am positive you would be welcomed on Homeworld and made comfortable there, both you and your family. It will not matter if you are human."

"But why change a good thing?" someone says, speaking up. It is Lila, the dark-haired one that had her hearing restored. Her mate has his hands on her shoulders, and she holds her son tightly. "I thank you for what you did for me and for saving Harlow. But I want nothing to change. I don't want to leave the people here, and I don't want to leave this place. It might not look much like Earth, but I like the snow. I like the culture. Most of all, I love the people. Nothing offered on either Earth or your homeworld is worth leaving that for.

I'm sorry. You're not going to find many takers."

"And you all agree?" Chatav glances at the crowd of gathered people. "Every one of you?"

Farli pulls herself from her mother's arms. She gives Kemli a sad look, but her mother just nods and squeezes her shoulder, as if telling her she understands. "I am going with you, Cap-tan," Farli says. "I wish to stay with Mardok."

Someone gasps. Her brothers look incredulous. "You are leaving, my daughter?" Borran says. He looks devastated.

The sick feeling of wrongness in my gut continues.

She turns to her father and clasps his hands. "Mardok is my mate, father. I resonated to him the moment we met."

"But if you leave, you will not have resonance to bind you together."

"I know. But it does not matter. We love each other and wish to be together, regardless."

"You must do what you feel in your heart is right, my daughter." Kemli puts her hand on Farli's arm. "We will miss you terribly, but you must walk your own path." Her smile wobbles. "Even if it is not with us."

"Oh, Mother, I will miss you!" Farli flings herself back into her mother's arms, sobbing. Her father and mother embrace her tightly, stroking her hair and whispering to her. Farli's three brothers look shocked, but they move to hug their sister as well. Soon, she is enveloped by the entire tribe, as each person wishes her goodbye.

She has made her choice, I remind myself. *It shouldn't feel wrong. Farli is an adult. You both want to be together.* But I can't get over the feeling that this isn't how it should go. I watch as she moves to her pet and hugs him one last time. She strokes his shaggy fur and murmurs to him, and the dvisti licks her face and bleats happily. She eventually moves away, heading back to my side, and he tries to follow. Kemli grabs the dvisti by the collar and pulls him back, and it looks as if Farli will start crying all over again.

I turn to Chatav. "Captain—"

"Before you ask, Vendasi," Chatav says in a cool voice. "That animal will never make it past quarantine. Better for it to remain here."

He's right, of course. Doesn't mean that it's not tearing my heart out to watch Farli have to give up everything and everyone she loves. Except me, of course.

The wrong feeling seems to be permanently lodged in my gut. I pull Farli into my arms and hold her close, pressing a kiss to her brow. She buries her face against my neck, and I can feel her tears freezing against the collar of my enviro-suit. I wish I could make this easier for her.

I wish she didn't have to do it at all. There's still time, though. I could change my mind. Stay behind with her. Let the ship leave me. Stranded. Again. The thought fills me with endless, deep terror, and I hold Farli tight.

"If you wish to remain, then I must honor your choice," Chatav says. "I do not understand it, but I honor it."

"Thank you," Vektal says, and clasps Chatav's hand. "You are welcome back to visit at any time, of course. My people will welcome you with open arms." His words are directed at Chatav, but I suspect they are for Farli.

"I do not think this is likely, Chief Vektal," Chatav says with a polite smile. "Your planet is out of the way of most shipping lanes. But I thank you for the offer. If there is nothing further, then we must be on our way."

There's nothing more to do or say. Farli gives her family another quick, tearful goodbye, and Chompy bleats miserably as we head back to the *Lady*. We are all silent as we ride up the pulley-platform, the only sound that of Farli's quiet crying. Niri makes an impatient sound, and I shoot her an incredulous look. Is she truly so heartless? Farli is losing everything. But the medic only rolls her eyes at me and crosses her arms over her chest.

And these are the people I am bringing Farli to live with. Gods help us both. They are cold and unfeeling down to a man, and Farli's warmth will be lost on them. Am I dooming her to unhappiness?

She takes my hand as we move toward the *Lady*, and her fingers are cold against mine. Her hand is trembling, and it is the first time I have ever felt Farli be afraid. I hate this. I hate everything about it. It feels wrong. Just flat-out wrong.

Farli and I are the last ones in the ship. She watches as the door closes slowly, her last glimpse of her icy home falling away to metal. Then the doors are closed and there's nothing more to see. Farli turns to me, and she tries to smile brightly, but I can tell she's hurting. I cup her face and kiss it gently. "I love you."

"Enough of that," Niri says, heading toward med bay. "I'll warm up the machines. Send her my way and I'll get that parasite out of her in no time."

Farli flinches. I do, too. A parasite. That's all it is to everyone else. To them, the khui isn't a helpful thing or something that chooses a mate. There's no reason to think there's a connection between two people other than biological. And yet... everyone in the village is happy with their khui-chosen mate. And Farli's khui has chosen me, and I've fallen in love with her in an incredibly short amount of time. It's like the thing wants what is truly best for her.

And she's giving everything up to be with me.

The thought of being left behind fills me with a sick terror, but the thought of letting the warmth and light inside of Farli be destroyed by taking her away? That decides it.

The engines start to power up. Trakan has to be starting

the ship. There's no reason to delay, not any longer. I need to act now. I move to the wall and grab the emergency alert handle and twist it. A klaxon sounds through the ship, alerting the bridge to abort the take-off. Farli looks at me in surprise, rubbing her ear at all the noise. "What is it, Mardok?"

I turn back to her, grabbing her by the shoulders. "Do you want to stay, Farli?"

Panic crosses her face. "I do not want to leave you—"

I correct her quickly. "That's not what I'm asking. Do you want to stay? Because if you want to stay, I'll stay with you."

She sucks in a breath, her eyes wide. "But that is your greatest fear, Mardok. Being left behind. I would not do that to you."

I take her hands in mine and bring them to my mouth, kissing her knuckles. "I think it would be worse to take you away and watch you be forced to change. I love who you are, Farli. I love that naked, wild girl that I met a few days ago. The one that put my hand on her breast and kissed me. The one that's carefree and unbroken by society's rules. And I think…I think leaving would be a mistake. I think it would crush who you are, and I love you too much for that to happen."

Tears shimmer in her glowing blue eyes. "But…what about you?"

I try to laugh, even though I'm choking with panic. "I'm gonna need my hand held for a few days, I think, until I get used to the concept of being left behind. But I think I can handle it, as long as I'm with you."

She flings her arms around my neck and kisses my face, over and over again. "Oh, Mardok! You would stay? Truly?"

"For you, I'll do anything—"

"What's going on?" Niri comes racing into the corridor, followed by Trakan and Chatav. She's got a fierce frown on her face. "What the kef, Vendasi?"

"I'm staying," I tell her bluntly. "I'm not taking Farli away from her world."

Niri gives me an incredulous look. "You can't be serious."

"I gotta second that, Vendasi," Trakan says. "You'd be crazy to stay. It's nothing but ice and snow. No cities, no nothing. There's nothing here."

That's where they're wrong. Farli's here. Her warm, loving people are here. There's a life for us together here, and a child. That's enough for me. I turn to Farli and smile, decided. "Shall we rejoin the others and give them the news?"

She hugs me again, her eyes brimming with joy instead of tears. "The tribe will celebrate! There will be a feast tonight in your honor."

All I really want to do is go back to her house and curl up with her, but I nod. "Feast sounds good. As long as I'm with you, everything's good."

Her hand clutches mine tightly, and she's radiant in her happiness. This is the right thing, I know it is.

"Well damn, if there's a party, I wanna stay another night, too," Trakan says. "We gotta send our boy off in style."

Chatav just sighs and rubs his brow. "Another delay?"

The last one. I won't be around for the next. I swallow the fear in my gut and hold Farli tightly.

IN THE END, THERE IS a party. A big party. The sa-khui tribe is overjoyed at Farli's return and my status as the newest tribesmate. I'm showered in hugs and given tunics and food and everything under the sun as housewarming presents. Plans are made for the morning—we'll be up early to hunt some big creature and get a khui for me. For some reason, I'm calm. I'm no longer panicked like I was before at the thought of being left behind. I'm not, not really. Everything's here. With

Farli at my side, I'm never truly going to be alone ever again. And while it's a little worrying to think about staying on this primal planet for the rest of my life, there are things to look forward to. I'll get to tinker with the Elders' Cave some more. I'll get to go on more hunts with Farli's brothers, and I might actually get good at it someday. If nothing else, I'd love to be half as athletic as them.

More than anything else, I'm looking forward to being with Farli, now and forever.

And, all right, I'm looking forward to impregnating her. What man in his right mind wouldn't?

The celebration is a rowdy one, and people drink lots of sah-sah. Trakan's got his head together with his buddies Bek and Vaza, I guess getting a few last-minute bootleg liquor deals in. Niri remained only briefly, then returned to the ship with a cursory hug for me. I wonder if we were ever friends or if I've just imagined it. Maybe Niri truly does need no one. The thought makes me a little sad.

Captain Chatav moves to my side and comes to sit next to me by the fire. He's silent, and I wait for him to reproach me. To lecture me on leaving him without a mechanic for the rest of the haul. But when he finally looks over at me, he nods. "You're doing the right thing."

"I am?" I'm surprised to hear that coming from him.

"Indeed. Look at how happy you've made her." He nods to Farli, who is sitting with her mother, painting a replica of my tattoo on her mother's arm. She glances over at me and gives me a radiant smile full of promise.

I can't help but grin back at her. I'm stupidly happy, too. I don't ever remember being quite so happy. "It feels like the right thing, you know? I don't have anyone waiting for me at home. Seemed wrong to pull her from everything she loves just because I don't like snow." I'm downplaying it a bit, of course, but Chatav doesn't need to know about my hang-ups. "Whatever the reason, I'm glad. You shouldn't end up a lonely old man like me."

And again, I'm surprised. "Did you have someone you left behind, Captain?"

His smile is faint. "Why do you think I made a career of the military? Once upon a time, there was nothing left for me, either." He gets to his feet and straightens his clothing. "I'm cold. I'm heading back to the *Lady*. Send Trakan up when he's done drinking, will you? We'll leave at first light in the morning."

He extends his hand to me.

I get to my feet and take it. "You're a good man, Captain."

"It's been an honor to serve with you, Vendasi." He smiles, and then adds, "Mardok."

And kef, I'm getting choked up. I grip his arm, full of respect for this man. "I've got a few years' pay saved up in my cabin. Box of credit chits stashed under my mattress. I want you to take it. It's not much, but it'll help pay for any problems with this shipment." I think for a moment, and then add, "And might want to give some to Niri. She's probably pissed that the tribe cleaned out some of her med bay supplies."

The captain nods. "Thank you."

He turns and leaves, and I watch him go. Like Niri, I wonder if I truly knew the man or if I've just been so wrapped up in my own head that I've pushed everyone away. Everyone except Farli. Too late to mend that now. Maybe I'll see the captain again someday. Probably not, but if I do, I'll buy him a drink and a meal.

Or since I'm going to be one of the local 'savages,' I guess I'll slaughter him a meal and brew him a drink. There are so many skills I need to learn here, but I'm looking forward to the challenge. As long as I have Farli, I'll be able to handle anything.

I look over at her, and she's now by Georgie's side, chatting and drawing a replica of my tattoos on Georgie's arm with a paintbrush and yellow paints. She glances up at me from across the fire, and a shy smile of delight curves her lovely mouth. My heart surges with joy at the sight of her. This is good. This feels right. This is where I'm meant to be—at her side, her mate. I make my way through the cluster of people near the fire and lean in to whisper in her ear. "Think we can get away without being disturbed?"

"Of course. Why?" Her eyes are full of amusement.

"Because I want to go and make a baby with you."

She jumps to her feet and flings her arms around my neck. "Let us go, then. And quickly."

Laughter bubbles up from the crowd. I grin as I pull my mate into my arms, carrying her. We've got a few hours before we have to be up for the big khui hunt in the morning, and I intend that we don't sleep for a single one.

BEK

"You're sure we can do this?" Trakan asks as I lead him through the thick snow toward the flashing red light in the distance.

"Positive," I tell him.

"But Mardok lost his shit when we tried to salvage the other ship. What makes this one so different?" Trakan glances back at Cap-tan, whose face is impassive.

I bite back my impatience, because I need this fool. "The other cave was the home of our elders. It means a great deal to my people. This?" I flick a dismissive hand at the wreck before us. "This is nothing but an intruder. No one comes here to salvage things or to commune with the ancestors. In a few seasons, it will be completely covered in snow and gone." I step past a frozen sky-claw carcass. "You said you wanted a cave like the Elders' Cave. I have brought you one."

"Another crashed ship," Trakan breathes as he follows close at my heels. "For a planet in the middle of nowhere, you guys sure do get a lot of play."

I do not know what he is talking about. I do not care, either. This is the cave-ship that brought Li-lah and Mah-dee. No one is attached to it. No one will care if it has been ransacked as these greedy ones wish to do.

"And you won't get in trouble for bringing us here?" The elder, Cap-tan, asks.

I shake my head. "They are off on a sa-kohtsk hunt and will be gone for many days. No one will notice I am gone." I lead the way inside the broken hull of the cave-ship. Snow has drifted inside, but I can see the remains of an old fire from many seasons ago. No one has been here since then. Even the animals and metlaks avoid it.

The two strangers wander inside, shining beams of light from their hands. Trakan whistles. "This looks like a szzt cruiser."

"It does," Cap-tan agrees.

"Salvage of the ship itself is a bad idea, then. A single registration number on this baby gets out and we're going to have every bounty hunter in the galaxy after our asses. Better to just see what we can take and go." Trakan glances at me. "Which way to the bridge?"

I frown, arms crossed over my chest. "Bridge?"

"Right. I keep forgetting. You probably don't know what that is. Never mind."

Cap-tan shines his light-beam onto the wall, where the

two pods were broken open. "Cryo chambers. Two open, the others empty. Slaving, you think?" He looks to Trakan.

"Only one reason for szzt to have cryo. Intelligent cargo."

I do not know what they are saying. "Two humans came from here. Are there more?" My heart gives an excited thump. Perhaps someone was missed?

But Cap-tan shakes his head. "Not likely."

I bite back my disappointment.

"What happened to the crew?" Cap-tan asks.

"Dead," I tell them. "One of the humans made sure they did not leave." I gesture up ahead, where the cave forks into narrower passageways. "They are in that direction."

"We need crew quarters," Trakan says, moving his beam in that direction. He heads inside and then tilts his head. "Think I found a dead guy here. Frozen solid." He bends down and pats the body. "Nothing worth taking."

"Mmm." I wait. Surely they will find something they want.

They do, some time later. They find a room with two strange chairs staring at a wall that is cracked into many pieces. Tiny buttons and sticks are laid out in front of them. "The bridge," Cap-tan murmurs. "And look. Under the station itself…"

Trakan's light-beam shines on a square on the floor. "Kef yeah. A blast-safe."

Their excitement is palpable, and mine rises. I wait silently as they poke and prod at the thing for the next while, until one of them attaches a small square to the front and pushes buttons. New lights shine, and something chirps a sequence. "What is that?" Cap-tan asks, and his voice is disapproving.

"Best if you don't ask, sir."

Cap-tan snorts. "I had better not see that used on the *Lady*, ever."

"No, sir." It chimes, and Trakan grins. "It's open."

Both men lean forward as the lid hisses up, and they shine their light-beams there. My curiosity rising, I look, too.

It is full of small boxes. It does not look exciting to me, but one of the men sucks in a breath. Trakan grabs the first box and pulls the lid off. "Kef," he breathes. "Credit chits. Hundreds of them. These fools crashed with a fortune on them." He pulls one out and flips it over, then looks at Cap-tan in excitement. "Nontraceable."

Cap-tan sags in obvious relief. "That is good. That is very, very good."

"This is your salvage?" I ask. "This is what you want?"

"This is amazing," Trakan says, grabbing another box. "We're keffing rich!"

I put a hand on his shoulder. "Good. I need something from you." Excitement rises through me, and I force my expression to remain calm.

Cap-tan's eyes narrow at me. "What is it you want? Credit chits are of no use to you here."

"I want none of this." I gesture at the cave-ship of the bad ones. "You can take all of it. I said I would take you here, and I did. But I want something in exchange for what you take. It is only fair."

"Whatever you want, name it," Trakan says.

Even Cap-tan does not hesitate. He nods. "Speak."

I choose my words carefully. It is something Vaza and I have discussed, ever since the newcomers arrived and Farli resonated. There is still a chance out there for us. "This ship carried humans."

"Slaves," Cap-tan agrees. "Illegal slaves."

"But there is a way to get more of them and bring them here." I pause, and then continue before they can object. "I want a mate. There is no female of suitable age for me. Not in our tribe. Not for myself, and not for the four other hunters that still wish for mates. I want you to bring back humans—these ee-lee-gull slaves you speak of—and bring them here. Five of them. We will take good care of them and make them good mates. They will be happy with us, like Shorshie and the others."

They exchange a look. "What you ask is not easy," Cap-tan says.

"That is my price."

He nods. "I will see what I can do."

EPILOGUE

MARDOK

"I DON'T FEEL ANY DIFFERENT," I tell Farli as we lie in our furs the next night. We are out in the open, our sleeping pallet piled close to the others. There is no fire, because all of the hunters who came with us are sa-khui and the symbiont keeps them warm.

And for the first time since arriving on this planet, I'm not cold. It's keffing amazing. The snow doesn't bother me. It just feels like damp powder, not icy hell. I curl up with Farli under the furs and pull her against me, and she doesn't feel hot to the touch, just pleasant.

"I like your eyes much better this way," she tells me, snuggling up to my chest. "Such a nice blue. Not dead like before."

"Dead?" I say with a laugh. "Really?"

"Very dark and no spark of life in them," she says with a nod. Her fingers trail up and down my chest. "And I am glad you have a khui."

I am, too. I thought I would feel strange, but I don't. I don't feel much of anything, except for the steady drumming song in my chest that started the moment I woke up and looked at Farli. Resonance. I expected it to fill me with a surge of emotion for her.

I didn't expect for it to make my cock stand at attention constantly. I guess it's the symbiont getting me ready to make babies with her. I guess we didn't try hard enough last night. I grin and pull her closer. I'm willing to give it as many tries as we need. Not right now, of course. Not with the others sleeping close nearby. Plenty of time for that when we return to the village and her cozy little house.

I gaze up at the stars overhead, my mate tucked against my shoulder. Somewhere up there, *The Tranquil Lady* is soaring away from this planet and toward her shipping destination. My seat is empty. Bron Mardok Vendasi will be listed as missing in space. My flight-suit has been sent out the airlock by now, and the others will do their best to cover my trail and make it seem like I'm just…gone. No one will come looking for me. Accidents happen in space all the time, and someone like me with a sad history? It wouldn't be too much to assume that I just went out the airlock while the others were sleeping.

I watched the ship leave earlier, during the hunt. The chaos of the moment and the chase of the enormous, dangerous creature meant that I didn't have time to focus on it leaving. There was no time to be anxious. No time for my mind to fray at the edges and think back to those awful days on Uzocar. No time to feel like I was left behind, because Farli was at my side, encouraging me to shove my spear— however awkwardly—into the flanks of the sa-kohtsk as it tumbled to the ground.

It was the first kill I participated on, and I felt a sense of pride when the others slapped my back in approval. Then there was no time to focus on anything except the khui itself, and receiving it. The moment the glowing filament touched my skin, I blacked out. I woke up later, warm and strangely content, and purring to Farli.

Of course, now that I have time to stare up at the sky and panic at the thought of being stranded here on Kopan VI forever? I'm oddly calm. The worst has happened, and I'm fine with it. I'm not on an enemy planet. I'm not forgotten. I'm here by choice. I've got an entire village of people who are warm and friendly and giving. I've got an ancient wreck of a ship to tinker with. Most of all, I have the woman I love at my side.

With her, I'm never going to be alone again.

AUTHOR'S NOTE

EEEE!

I have wanted to write Farli's book for a YEAR. No joke. The moment Harlow started tinkering with the Elders' ship, I knew that someone from Homeworld was going to come back and Farli was going to resonate to him. Some books pop into your mind with complete plots, and this one did. It was a joy to write, not only because Farli's so forthright and happy, but because Mardok's so stoically wounded on the inside and trying to hide it. I know a lot of people were Team Bek but I've never seen him with Farli. I hope you see why!

And I hope you can guess where the next few books are going. I think you'll like how we're heading. I do get asked a lot if there will be more books. My answer — I have plans for books for at least four more. Provided that sales remain strong, I'm ready to keep going if you guys are ready to keep reading.

A few notes about this book in particular. Mardok and his civilization are extremely advanced, and have completely different language patterns, customs, everything. It quickly got overwhelming for me mentally to determine how much I should pepper into the book. I'm more about giving the reader an immersive, enjoyable experience than being 100% technically correct. So Mardok has a bit of his own slang tossed in (keffing!) and a lot of our own idioms in there simply because it makes the book flow. Some of you might be out there saying, "An advanced culture wouldn't talk like this, Ruby!" And I know this! But I thought it would 'keep you in the story' more than a phrase like "Mardok picked up his *zabiji* and gave the *kislani* a toss. *Bazet milani,* he hated when the *zippi doo dat* had a *yippie-ki-yay* stuck into it." See what I mean? It drives me crazy as a reader (and it's like wading through mud as a writer) so I opted for a more conversational tone.

Speaking of conversational tones, I've also updated a few of the barbarian words. You'll notice that Farli uses 'village' instead of 'vee-lage' and 'house' instead of 'howse'. This was a slippery slope and I worried that, a few more books in, we'd have an entire quasi-language that would make it hell for casual readers to follow. I like to think that after a few years of using the human words, they're easier on the mouth. Maybe we'll migrate the names over, too (though I find them charming as they are).

The tribal list has also been updated! In addition to a bunch of new kits on the block, I've also updated a few small familial connections, like Bek and Maylak being related, and Zennek being the brother of Farli & co.

See, there's a method to my madness!

And all of that minutiae was probably extremely boring for some of you to read. Sorry not sorry! It's a living, breathing tribe in my head — and from the messages I get on Facebook, I'm not the only one. I'm so thrilled that everyone's still having fun on this journey with me. You guys are fantastic fans and I've been having a blast with these books. The series itself is getting long and in my brain, Farli's book is the 'end' of a cycle. That doesn't mean that there won't be more books. There will be! It just means they might have slightly different covers/titles but it'll still be the tribe we know and love and the hunters that are so desperately awaiting their mates.

Much love <3
— Ruby

THE PEOPLE OF ICE PLANET BARBARIANS

As of the end of Barbarian's Choice
(8 years post human landing)

Mated couples and their kits

Vektal (Vehk-tall) – The chief of the sa-khui. Mated to Georgie.

Georgie – Human woman (and unofficial leader of the human females). Has taken on a dual-leadership role with her mate. The sa-khui cannot pronounce her name correctly and refer to her as 'Shorshie'.

Talie (Tah-lee) – Their first daughter.

Vekka (Veh-kah) – Their second daughter.

Maylak (May-lack) – Tribe healer. Mated to Kashrem. Sister to Bek.

Kashrem (Cash-rehm) - Her mate, also a leather-worker.

Esha (Esh-uh) – Their teenage daughter.

Makash (Muh-cash) — Their younger son.

Sevvah (Sev-uh) – Tribe elder, mother to Aehako, Rokan, and Sessah
Oshen (Aw-shen) – Tribe elder, her mate
Sessah (Ses-uh) - Their youngest son

Ereven (Air-uh-ven) Hunter, mated to Claire
Claire – Mated to Ereven
Erevair (Air-uh-vair) - Their first child, a son
Relvi (Rell-vee) – Their second child, a daughter

Liz – Raahosh's mate and huntress.
Raahosh (Rah-hosh) – Her mate. A hunter and brother to Rukh.
Raashel (Rah-shel) – Their daughter.
Aayla (Ay-lah) – Their second daughter

Stacy – Mated to Pashov. Unofficial tribe cook.
Pashov (Pah-showv) – son of Kemli and Borran, brother to Farli, Zennek, and Salukh. Mate of Stacy.
Pacy (Pay-see) – Their first son.
Tash (Tash) – Their second son.

Nora – Mate to Dagesh. Currently pregnant after a second resonance.
Dagesh (Dah-zhesh) (the g sound is swallowed) – Her mate. A hunter.
Anna & Elsa – Their twin daughters.

Harlow – Mate to Rukh. Once 'mechanic' to the Elders' Cave. Currently pregnant after a second resonance.

Rukh (Rookh) – Former exile and loner. Original name Maarukh. (Mah-rookh). Brother to Raahosh. Mate to Harlow.

Rukhar (Roo-car) – Their infant son.

Megan – Mate to Cashol. Mother to newborn Holvek.

Cashol (Cash-awl) – Mate to Megan. Hunter. Father to newborn Holvek.

Holvek (Haul-vehk) – their infant son.

Marlene (Mar-lenn) – Human mate to Zennek. French.

Zennek (Zehn-eck) – Mate to Marlene. Father to Zalene. Brother to Pashov, Salukh, and Farli.

Zalene (Zah-lenn) – daughter to Marlene and Zennek.

Ariana – Human female. Mate to Zolaya. Currently pregnant. Basic school 'teacher' to tribal kits.

Zolaya (Zoh-lay-uh) – Hunter and mate to Ariana. Father to Analay.

Analay (Ah-nuh-lay) – Their son.

Tiffany – Human female. Mated to Salukh. Tribal botanist.

Salukh (Sah-luke) – Hunter. Son of Kemli and Borran, brother to Farli, Zennek, and Pashov.

Lukti (Lookh-tee) – Their son.

Aehako (Eye-ha-koh) – Acting leader of the South cave. Mate to Kira, father to Kae. Son of Sevvah and Oshen, brother to Rokan and Sessah.

Kira – Human woman, mate to Aehako, mother of Kae. Was the first to be abducted by aliens and wore an ear-translator for a long time.

Kae (Ki –rhymes with 'fly') – Their newborn daughter.

Kemli (Kemm-lee) – Female elder, mother to Salukh, Pashov, Zennek, and Farli. Tribe herbalist.

Borran (Bore-awn) – Her mate, elder. Tribe brewer.

Josie – Human woman. Mated to Haeden. Currently pregnant for a third time.

Haeden (Hi-den) – Hunter. Previously resonated to Zalah, but she died (along with his khui) in the khui-sickness before resonance could be completed. Now mated to Josie.

Joden (Joe-den) – Their first child, a son.

Joha (Joe-hah) – Their second child, a daughter.

Rokan (Row-can) – Oldest son to Sevvah and Oshen. Brother to Aehako and Sessah. Adult male hunter. Now mated to Lila. Has 'sixth' sense.

Lila – Maddie's sister. Once hearing impaired, recently reacquired on The Tranquil Lady via med bay. Resonated to Rokan. Currently pregnant for a second time.

Rollan (Row-lun) – Their first child, a son.

Hassen (Hass-en) – Hunter. Previously exiled. Newly mated to Maddie.

Maddie – Lila's sister. Found in second crash. Newly mated to Hassen.

Masan (Mah-senn) – Their son.

Asha (Ah-shuh) – Mate to Hemalo. Mother to Hashala (deceased) and Shema.

Hemalo (Hee-muh-low) – Mate to Asha. Father to Hashala (deceased) and Shema.

Shema (Shee-muh) – Their daughter.

Farli – (Far-lee) Adult daughter to Kemli and Borran. Her brothers are Salukh, Zennek, and Pashov. She has a pet dvisti named Chompy (Chahm-pee). Mated to Mardok.

Mardok (Marr-dock) – Bron Mardok Vendasi, from the planet Ubeduc VII. Arrived on The Tranquil Lady. Mechanic and ex-soldier. Resonated to Farli and elected to stay behind.

Unmated Elders

Drayan (Dry-ann) – Elder.
Drenol (Dree-nowl) – Elder.
Vadren (Vaw-dren) – Elder.
Vaza (Vaw-zhuh) – Widower and elder. Loves to creep on the ladies.

Unmated Hunters

Bek – (Behk) – Hunter. Brother to Maylak.

Harrec (Hair-ek) – Hunter.

Taushen (Tow – rhymes with cow – shen) – Hunter.

Warrek (War-ehk) – Tribal hunter and teacher. Son to Eklan (now deceased).

Made in the USA
Las Vegas, NV
01 January 2025

15642539R40132